WHO FRAMED ROGER RABBIT™

A novel

Based on the Motion Picture from
Touchstone Pictures and Steven Spielberg

'THE BEST, PUREST MOTION PICTURE FANTASY
SINCE E.T.'

New York Times

'IT'S A SIGHT YOU WON'T WANT TO MISS'

Newsweek

'I'VE NEVER SEEN ANYTHING LIKE IT
BEFORE...'

New York Post

'IT'S THE MOST DAZZLING, MOST EXCITING,
MOST ENTERTAINING, MOST ORIGINAL AND
MOST BRILLIANTLY CONCEIVED AND
EXECUTED MOVIE I'VE SEEN IN YEARS'

At the Movies

'A COMPLEX, BEAUTIFUL WORK OF ART'

New York Newsday

D1493134

Who framed ROGER RABBIT

A novel by Martin Noble

Based on the Motion Picture from
Touchstone Pictures and Steven Spielberg
Executive Producers: Steven Spielberg, Kathleen Kennedy
Produced by Robert Watts & Frank Marshall
Screenplay by Jeffrey Price & Peter Seaman
Based on the Book *Who Censored Roger Rabbit?*
by Gary K. Wolf

A STAR BOOK
published by
the Paperback Division of
W.H. ALLEN & Co. Plc

A Star Book
Published in 1988
by the Paperback Division of
W.H. Allen & Co. Plc
44 Hill Street, London W1X 8LB

Printed in Great Britain by
Cox & Wyman Ltd,
Reading, Berks.

ISBN 0 352 32389 2

Who framed ROGER RABBIT™

1

It's Cartoon Time!

Hi, folks! Grab hold of your popcorn, tighten your seat belts and settle down: we're off on another side-splitting rip-roaring ride with everyone's favourite cartoon caperers. But just a word of caution: when you see that famous circular logo –

R. K. Maroon Presents

A MAROON CARTOON

you'd better make sure your heart's in good condition 'cos otherwise we're going to KILL you with laughter and this cinema will not – positively not – accept liability in cases of death by Toons. Seriously, folks – but let's face it, who can be serious when Toons are around! – it's those maestros of movie magic and mirth: the one and only zany King of Clowns, Carrots, Klutz, Corn and Comedy, Roger Rabbit and his cartoon pal, Toontown's smallest but sweetest star, Baby Herman, back together again in what director Raoul J. Raoul promises to be their funniest yet. So dim the lights, roll the projector, turn on the heat a little – and let's cook . . .

Somethin's Cookin'

'Goo goo gah gah,' says Baby Herman, looking meltingly up at his mother as she leans down to his living-room playpen and pats his head.

'Mommy's going to the beauty parlor, darling,' says Mrs Herman, 'but I'm leaving you with your favourite friend, Roger Rabbit.'

'Gurgle, gurgle coo.'

Across the living-room carpet walks Mrs Herman and we follow her legs in their elegant white high-heeled shoes to where Roger Rabbit lies asleep in the corner, next to a table.

'He's going to take very, very good care of you,' she says sweetly, pointing at Roger who blearily wakes up, 'because if he doesn't he's –' she presses her finger in his nose and adds, harshly '– GOING BACK TO THE SCIENCE LAB!'

'P-p-p-p-p-please!' splutters Roger Rabbit sheepishly, grovelling at her feet as she steps round him to the front door. 'Don't worry. Whatever you say! Yes, ma'am! Aye, aye, sir! Okie-dokie!' His huge floppy ears flap like loose sails. 'Why, I'll take care of him like he was my own brother. Or my own sister. Ouuch!'

'Gah goo gah goo gah goo,' babbles Baby Herman in his playpen.

Roger has accidentally banged his shiny red nose in the door as Mrs Herman slams it behind her. Undaunted, that goofy old rabbit continues to expand on the theme of his great big family. (We all know what rabbits do best, don't we folks?) 'Or my brother's sister. Or my second cousin...'

Baby Herman's angelic blue eyes gaze upwards beyond his playpen towards the kitchen and a gleam of delight animates them.

'... who is twice removed on my father's side.'

'Cookie,' sighs Baby Herman in rapture.

Roger Rabbit is counting on his fingers. 'Or my ninth cousin who is nine times removed from his place outside.'

Uh-oh... To illustrate his genealogical lecture our funny bunny is swinging his arms, first outwards to indicate the

2

wonderful miracle of rabbit procreation and then inwards to relocate himself at the centre of this rapidly growing family tree – and gets his arms all tangled up.

Lovable Baby Herman meanwhile is struggling to squeeze through the bars of his playpen.

Roger's lisp is getting thicker: 'Or like my sixteenth cousin who is sixteen times . . .'

With a massive effort for such a tiny cartoon character, Baby Herman pulls open the iron bars of his playpen: they snap back again, catapulting him up into the air, out of the living-room and into the kitchen.

'Cookie!'

Baby Herman lands neatly on the cartoon-clean, shiny, black-and-white-checked kitchen lino and slides on his cutely diapered little baby bottom over to the bottom of the fridge.

'. . . who is thirty-seven times removed from his father's side . . .'

Baby's blue-eyed gaze is now aimed vertically upwards at the large inviting cookie jar sitting on top of the fridge.

'Ahh! Cookie!'

'. . . who is eleven times removed from his fifty-sixth cousin's side,' continues Roger Rabbit, his fingers, hands, arms and brain now completely entangled in calculation.

'Coo-keee!'

'Or like my seventeenth cousin who is 156 times removed from any side!'

He is brought back to Toonland by a deafening crash. Untangling himself he peruses the playpen.

It is empty.

Looking across to the kitchen Roger Rabbit's eyes widen as he sees Baby Herman going on a mountaineering expedition up a chest of kitchen drawers, levering himself upwards on piton drawer handles and spilling out the contents of the drawers on his progress to the summit. As Baby reaches the top drawer an assortment of whisks, baking trays, knives, forks and spoons crash to the floor in a miniature avalanche.

'Aa-a-a-a-a . . .' shrieks Roger Rabbit, his eyes bulging as he leaps up into the air.

Meanwhile Baby Herman has moved off from first base and is beginning to crawl over the stove; as he does so, he turns on the burners with his cutesy-wootsy little dangling foot.

'... aa-ahhh!' yells Roger Rabbit, taking in the scene. He starts to make a run for the kitchen but something is holding him back and he finds himself running on the spot.

'I'll save you, Baby-y-y-y-y!' he cries, looking down to see that his feet have got caught in the bunched-up rug. With a stupendous leap, he extricates himself from the rug and shoots off towards the kitchen, his bow-tie – I bet you've seen *this* one before, folks! – hovering momentarily in the air where he has just been standing before whizzing off to catch up with him.

Baby Herman is now busily negotiating a precipitous path across the kitchen counter, knocking over a rolling-pin that is blocking his remorseless progress.

'Cookie!'

'Don't burn yourself, Baby Herman!' shrieks Roger Rabbit as he runs into the kitchen and – wouldn't you know it! – trips on the rolling-pin.

'Oh! What! W-w-w-w-whoa!'

For seconds he balances on the rolling pin as it rolls first this way, then that way, along the kitchen floor, while Baby Herman, just out of his reach, crawls across the counter. Roger makes a desperate lunge for him – and misses as the rolling pin goes spinning around the floor, carrying Roger along with it on a demented roller-skating figure-of-eight, until he is doing a ferocious pirouette in the middle of the floor.

'Wha-a-a! Whoa! Wha-a-a-a ...'

At last he parts company with the rolling pin and renews his attempts to rescue Baby Herman – who accidentally kicks a large teapot off the counter. The teapot drops on Roger Rabbit.

'Ah-uggh!' comes Roger's muffled voice as his head, and half his ears, disappear inside the teapot. 'Who turned out the lights?'

He circles the kitchen awkwardly as though playing Blind Man's Buff, his voice making a dull echo inside the teapot. 'Boy, it's dark in here. Didn't they ...'

Blissfully unconcerned, Baby Herman is crawling over the 'Hotternell' brand oven and – you've guessed it! – accidentally kicks open the oven door just as poor old Roger Rabbit is stumbling towards it.

'. . . pay their electricity?'

The oven door slams shut – with Roger Rabbit inside it.

Uh, oh! That little rascal Baby Herman is on the move again and now his tiny wandering toes have accidentally landed on the oven knob, which naturally enough means that instead of registering 'OFF', the knob now reads 'ON' – it looks like Mrs Herman is going to have rabbit pie for dinner.

'What happened?' comes Roger Rabbit's muffled voice from inside the oven. 'I'll find you, Baby. Where are . . .'

The knob moves past 'ON' to 'HOT' as Baby Herman's foot slips again, and now a sign underneath lights up:

'VOLCANO HEAT'

As Baby Herman crawls ever onwards over piles of dishes in the sink, his eyes still fixed on the cookie jar above him, smoke begins to trickle out of the sides of the oven.

'. . . you?' Roger's question, which began almost rhetorically, ends in a note of genuine confusion. Then, even more to the point: 'Where am I?'

'Ooh, cookie,' gurgles Baby Herman, his eyes attracted to the pendulum of a cuckoo clock on the wall.

'What's that smoke?' gasps Roger Rabbit.

He is answered by a gurgle as Baby Herman slips on the dishes and tumbles into the dishwater.

'Boy, it's hot!' comes Roger's voice hoarsely from the oven as great black clouds of smoke start to billow out of it.

Baby Herman's pink little head pops up from the water and a podgy arm reaches unsuccessfully for the pendulum, accidentally flipping on the water tap *en route*.

'Oh!' he chuckles happily.

'Oh, it's so hot,' Roger Rabbit chokes. 'I smell something . . .'

Water begins to overflow from the sink and pour out over

the edge of the counter, carrying with it a bar of soap, while the billows of smoke from the oven are quickly fogging up the kitchen.

'... burning,' Roger perseveres. 'I'm on ...'

The oven knob changes from 'VOLCANO HEAT' to 'WELL DONE'.

'... fire! Whoa! Whoa! It's too hot.'

In the same instant, a timer alarm rings: the oven door falls open and a lump of smoking charcoal with a teapot on its head bursts out.

'Aaggh!' screams Roger Rabbit as he flies through the air and lands on the floor. Then, like a smoke bomb on legs, he runs round and round the kitchen, a spiral of smoke trailing after him.

Baby Herman, meanwhile, has found a box labelled 'Deadly Mouse Poison', upon which he steps to enable him to reach once more for the cuckoo clock pendulum.

'Gah gah, cookie.'

Splat! Roger Rabbit's foot slips on the bar of soap, sending him flying straight up into the air, smoke still streaming from his burning tail, while the soap shoots off at an angle towards an ironing board that is folded up into the wall. With the kind of deadly precision that can only happen in cartoon movies the soap hits the latch on the ironing board, ricochets off and flies back in the direction of Baby Herman.

Baby is still standing on the box of mouse poison as the soap bounces on his bottom. With a sigh, he is lifted a few inches up into the air – just high enough for him to grab hold of the clock pendulum.

As Baby begins to swing from the pendulum Roger goes crashing back to the floor, which is now flooded with dish- and tap-water.

Where exactly does he land? Why, on the soap, of course, and as he goes skidding across the floor on the wet soap he sticks out his fingers to protect himself from crashing into the wall.

Sure enough, his fingers meet the wall before he does – or, more accurately, they meet a couple of electrical sockets placed conveniently at floor level.

A split second after his fingers plunge into the sockets, a bolt of electricity shoots through him, lighting up his rabbitty skeleton. He begins to pound his head – still stuck inside the teapot – against the wall, and the plaster starts to crack.

Above him there is a shelf piled high with pots and pans and as the crack widens and makes its way up the wall it loosens the shelf support until, with a shudder, the shelf tips over and the pans come tumbling down, crashing on Roger Rabbit's teapot-covered head; jerked out of his catatonia he yanks his hands back out of the sockets and falls unconscious to the waterlogged kitchen floor.

The last of the pots and pans slide off the broken shelf, to reveal a bottle marked 'Chile Sauce – Extra Hot'. For a few moments the bottle hesitates, balancing precariously on the edge of the shelf. Maybe it's wondering whether this isn't just a little bit over the top even for a Roger Rabbit and Baby Herman cartoon. Then, almost with a sigh, it gives in and goes over the top . . . planting itself squarely on the spout of the teapot which starts to turn bright red as Roger Rabbit gulps down the sauce.

'Uggggghhhhh!' Roger gurgles.

'Cookie. Ooh,' Baby Herman sighs as he swings on the clock pendulum.

'Whoo-whoo-whoo . . .' Roger wails, his body quivering violently as steam shoots out of his pores. '. . . whoo-whoo-whoo-whoo-whoo-whoo!'

The teapot starts to whistle and soon reaches boiling point: with a blast of steam it shoots Roger out like a bullet.

He flies once more through the air, this time towards the unlatched ironing board which chooses this moment to drop, impaling Roger Rabbit through his gaping mouth before snapping back up into the wall, taking Roger with it.

Meanwhile Baby Herman is merrily catapulting himself off the pendulum and on to a small shelf conveniently perched above a dish drainer on the counter below, into which has been placed every type of kitchen knife imaginable.

'Cookie,' gurgles Baby Herman, dangling by one hand from

7

the shelf and reaching up with his other for the cookie jar.

There is a noise of something tearing.

The flimsy little shelf from which Baby Herman is hanging breaks under his weight. With a gentle, cooing sound, Baby falls on to a sink plunger, at the same time as a jar of pickles slides off the shelf and on to the edge of the dish drainer.

Like a fleet of jet fighters working to precisely coordinated and pre-planned instructions, the entire batch of knives whizzes off into the air . . .

It's Baby Herman's lucky day. The bouncing handle of the plunger flings him up towards the fridge, while the plunger itself flies off in the opposite direction. Landing on a pile of bread on top of the fridge Baby grabs hold of the cookie jar.

'Hee hee, cookie, gurgle goo,' he giggles.

The ironing board falls open to reveal Roger Rabbit, wonder of wonders, standing on it, as fresh as a daisy. That's the magic of movies.

(But let us not forget the knives which even now are *en route* to their target; nor the plunger: tumbling through the air it has bumped into a toaster.)

'I'm here, Bab –' he begins – and then screams as the armada of knives home in on their target, namely Roger Rabbit, pinning him to the wall. One particularly brutal-looking butcher's knife barely misses his groin.

Roger stares at the knives and down at his groin – and gulps.

At the same moment the toaster falls over, shooting out the plunger, which makes a beeline for Roger Rabbit, fixing itself firmly to his face.

'Just don't –' comes a muffled voice from inside the plunger.

On top of the fridge Baby Herman is standing on the pile of bread, kicking off one slice after another as he struggles to reach the cookie jar.

'– worry, Baby,' Roger Rabbit splutters as Baby Herman gurgles and babbles to himself. 'I'm right here!'

He puffs and pants, straining to pull the plunger off his face.

'Talk about suction.'

'Cookie, goo gah.'

'This is –' Roger Rabbit mutters as, still struggling against the tenacious plunger, he finally yanks himself free of the knives, off the wall – and flies through the air, with the plunger still glued to his face.

'– ridiculous.'

'Gah, gah, hee hee, cookie.'

'Don't worry, Baby Herman!' Roger persists heroically, grunting and groaning until finally his efforts are rewarded: the plunger releases its grip and Roger cannot resist taking a look into the camera and grinning modestly to his millions of fans. Then he turns back and collides with the suction hose of a 'Suck-O-Lux' vacuum cleaner and, trust Roger Rabbit, he accidentally turns it on.

'Wha-a-a . . .'

The vacuum cleaner instantly inflates Roger's body into a grotesque balloon shape which starts to float up into the air.

Up on the fridge Baby Herman has kicked off the last piece of bread and finally pulls a cookie out of the jar.

'Cookie,' he cooes triumphantly.

Roger Rabbit, having inflated to peak capacity, pops off the vacuum cleaner and, with a sound like wind being released, whizzes around the kitchen like a balloon as he deflates.

'Wha-a-a-a-a-a-a!'

He smashes into the sink full of dishes, soars back up to the ceiling, bounces on several walls and finally careers into the bottom of the fridge, as Baby Herman peers down at him from the top with mild infantile curiosity.

'Bl-bl-bl-bl-bl-bl-bl-bl-bl-bl-bl-' goes Roger Rabbit like a helicopter running out of power as his head disappears under the refrigerator.

Baby Herman is leaning over the fridge trying to work out what has happened to Roger Rabbit's head, while Roger, jerking and groaning as he tries to get clear of the fridge, only succeeds in pulling himself – with the fridge still on top of his head – into the middle of the kitchen floor.

The movement is just enough to dislodge Baby Herman, who comes tumbling down, landing with a thud on Roger Rabbit's stomach.

'Oh!' says Baby Herman.

'Ugghh!' grunts Roger Rabbit.

But the shock of the landing allows Roger to lift the fridge clear of his head. Without a second thought, he lets go of the fridge to pick up Baby Herman.

'Cookie. Ah!' Baby sighs.

Kerplunk!

The fridge crashes down on Roger Rabbit's head again and the fridge door swings open to reveal Roger's head poking up through a hole in the bottom. He is in a complete daze and a circle of tiny birds are flying and tweeting around his head –

'Cut!'

Raoul J. Raoul, live action director of *Somethin's Cookin'* could barely contain his fury.

'All right,' shouted the assistant director to the crew. 'That's the shot.'

The two cartoon actors relaxed and the crew began talking among themselves, though the cheerfully demented pre-recorded cartoon music carried on.

'Cut! Cut! Cut!' Raoul groaned, walking up to the fridge inside which Roger Rabbit's head was still lodged, though he had clearly come out of his daze and was looking rather pleased with himself. Wasting no time, the director slapped the startled Toon across the head, while Baby Herman stood up, put his hands on his hips and yelled angrily at the director in a deep rasping voice, the voice of a seasoned adult actor who habitually smoked cigars between bottle feeds.

'What the hell was wrong with that take?' grumbled Baby Herman.

Even though it was graphically clear that Baby Herman was not only a baby but also, like Roger Rabbit, a living, walking cartoon – in other words, a Toon – here was one baby that wasn't going to be messed around by some two-bit director like Raoul J. Raoul.

'Nothing with you,' Raoul soothed his star baby Toon. 'You were great. You were perfect! You were better than perfect!' He looked back disdainfully at the fridge. 'It's Roger. He keeps blowin' his lines! Roger?'

As Baby muttered angrily to himself about havin
his time acting with amateurs, Raoul turned to the ra
and grabbed one of the Toon birds that was still flyi
his head.

'What's this?' he said angrily.

'A tweeting bird?' said Roger a little hesitantly.

The director shook his head in disbelief. 'A tweeting bird!'
He threw down the cartoon bird in disgust. It squawked a
couple of times and toddled away, looking confused.

'Roger, read the script!' Raoul said wearily, picking up a
shooting script from the floor and holding it out to the
mortified rabbit. 'It says, "Rabbit gets clunked. Rabbit sees
stars." Not *birds* – STARS!'

'That rabbit can't do anything right,' muttered Baby
Herman. 'I am so sick of this!' He glanced back at Roger, still
inside the fridge. 'That stupid damn rabbit!'

'Can we lose the playback, please!' Raoul said to the
assistant director.

'Stop the playback,' echoed the assistant director to the
sound engineer.

Abruptly the cartoon music stopped.

'I'm sick of this!' Baby grumbled.

Raoul turned back to Roger Rabbit. 'You're killin' me!' he
growled. 'Killin' me!' He winced and clutched at his stomach.
It was true what they said. Directing Toons was guaranteed to
give you an ulcer. He stormed off to take an Alka-Seltzer.

The wretched rabbit now really did look as though a fridge
had been dropped on him.

'For cryin' out loud, Roger!' said Baby Herman. 'How the
hell many times do we have to do this damn scene?' He toddled
off the kitchen set, threading his way through the camera crew
and barking over his shoulder at the director, 'Raoul, I'll be in
my trailer! Takin' a nap!'

There was a sudden shriek.

'Excuse me, toots,' Baby growled at the script girl whose
skirt he had just pulled up as he walked between her legs.

The director put down the glass of Alka-Seltzer and got up
from his chair.

11

'My stomach can't take this,' he muttered. 'This set is a mess. Clean this set up!' he added to a couple of crewmen who obediently began mop-up operations around the devastated kitchen.

'And get him out of there,' Raoul added, pointing at Roger Rabbit who was still stuck in the fridge. 'Or seal him up in it! Lose the lights! And say "Lunch!"' he added to the assistant director.

'Lu-u-u-u-nch!' echoed the assistant director and the crew began breaking up.

'That's lunch,' said Raoul, taking his jacket from his chair. 'We're on a half!'

Desperately Roger Rabbit scrambled out of the refrigerator and ran after him.

'Please, Raoul!' he beseeched, 'I can give you stars!'

Raoul quickened his pace and didn't turn.

'Just drop the refrigerator on my head one more time,' Roger pleaded, grabbing the director's jacket.

Raoul stopped in his tracks.

'Roger,' he said, fighting to keep his patience, 'I dropped it on your head twenty-three times already!'

He turned and continued walking but Roger stopped him again.

'I can take it!' Roger said bravely. 'Don't worry about me!'

Raoul sighed. 'I'm not worried about *you*. I'm worried about the refrigerator!'

He tugged his jacket out of the Toon's grasp and stormed off towards his trailer.

Frantic, Roger grabbed a frying pan from a crew member who happened to be passing with a box of props and ran off in pursuit.

'I can give you stars!' he repeated desperately. 'Look!'

He hit himself with the frying pan and a shoal of green, fishlike cartoon squiggles emanated from his head.

But they weren't stars.

In any case, Raoul hadn't bothered to turn. Ignoring the clashing and clanging as frying pan hit rabbit's head he disappeared into his trailer.

Nothing daunted, Roger tried again, hitting his head even harder.

'Look!'

This time a jingling spray of cartoon bells encircled his head.

'Loo-o-o-k!'

He had parked himself outside Raoul's trailer where he now proceeded to hit himself on the head with the frying pan in as many different ways as he could think of. Had Raoul been watching, which he wasn't, he would have had to admit that some of the results were extraordinary: miniature sheep, goldfish, potatoes, golf balls, carrots appeared in quick cartoon succession – but still no stars.

Raoul may not have been watching, but there was someone else who was – with obvious distaste – a short, stocky man wearing a striped shirt, a crumpled suit with double-breasted jacket and dark-brown Fedora hat. He had the kind of face with dark, burning eyes that would have made him perfect casting for the role of a small-time gangster in those pre-war Hollywood gangster movies of the thirties – a hitman for Bogart, Cagney or Raft. But the world – and Hollywood – had moved on from the golden era of the thirties.

This was Hollywood, 1947: all the old-time gangsters were long gone. All around the world life was returning to normal after the biggest global war in history and Hollywood had the perfect antidote: Toons...

'Please, Raoul,' Roger Rabbit was still begging. 'I can do it, I swear. Just give me another chance.'

'No, that was the last time, Rabbit,' came the director's voice from inside his trailer.

'But come on, Raoul, you don't understand.'

The man in the rumpled suit pulled a face, then reached into his shoulder holster and brought out a square pint bottle of whiskey.

He took a swig and grimaced, shaking his head.

'Toons,' sighed Eddie Valiant, as though that one word summed up all the madness of the world.

Which, of course, it did.

13

2

I should have smelled a rat when I got the call from Maroon's secretary.

There are two things in the world I'd learned not to trust: Toons and movie moguls. Especially if the latter happens to go by the name of R.K. Maroon.

But when you're down to your last couple of dimes, that's when your rat-smelling equipment doesn't function too good. In my experience anyway.

As for Toons... well, a Toon killed my brother. Now all that was left of him was half a nameplate – Valiant and Valiant, Private Detectives. We'd started up in '38 – 'TWO FLAT-FOOTS & A FLOOZY GO INTO BUSINESS', as the *Los Angeles Chronicle* had headlined it at the time. The floozy? That was Dolores. She was still around and doing fine, working up at the local bar, waitress, barmaid, a shoulder to cry on, everyone's friend. And she was. She was one of those dames you could talk to and not get tired of the sound of her voice or the look of her face or the shape of her body. Which was kind of curvy. I've always had a weakness for curves when they're wrapped round a heart of gold – or a pint of Scotch.

Now I must say here that things hadn't been looking too

good for me and Dolores around this time. You see, me and Teddy, my brother, we'd somehow got ourselves a reputation around Hollywood for helping Toons out of scrapes. It had all started when we had got Goofy out of a spy rap. After that, I guess it snowballed. Friends of the Toons, we had come to be known as. Until a Toon murdered Teddy. After that, I vowed never to help another Toon.

Trouble was, no Toons, no business. Nobody else would touch me. It was a mystery to me at the time, though it's pretty clear now what was going on. Anyway, I was down to borrowing money from Dolores. And drinking more whiskey than was good, even for me. Too much booze and no clients, and precious little of Dolores – that was my problem lately. And that brings me back to my non-functioning rat-smelling equipment and a rat called R.K. Maroon.

His office was typical pre-war Hollywood schmaltz, all art deco armchairs and walls littered with photos of the great man shaking hands with presidents, actresses and Toons.

I waited in an ante-room and could see him and one of his film editors standing over a moviola.

'He'll be right with you,' said his secretary, one of those tall platinum blondes who look down at you like you're something unpleasant they've accidentally stepped on in a dark alley – well, I guess I'm not exactly on the tall side so maybe it's just my paranoia.

'No! No! No!' I could hear Maroon shouting. 'Wait until he gets to his feet, then hit him with the boulder.'

'Right R.K.,' his editor was saying as I was ushered in. The minion pulled the film out of the moviola and disappeared into a cutting-room, leaving me alone with Maroon.

He stood with his back to me, then swung round in what I took to be a well-rehearsed intimidating tactic. I'd thought we'd seen the last of Mussolini and his like, but they just kept popping out of the woodwork.

The first thing I noticed was the maroon silk handkerchief folded neatly in his top pocket. The suit itself probably cost more than I had earned in the past two years – and his hair was polished with some expensive-smelling goo. I could see that he had the paunchy kind of face and physique of a man who ate and drank too much – and had bad dreams. There were deep bags under his eyes. He looked like a dog who never got to be taken for a walk. I wouldn't like to be in his kennel. It made me wonder, not for the first time, whether I should cut down on the whiskey, but then again I could have done with a shot at that moment.

'How much do you know about show business, Mr Valiant?' he demanded.

I shrugged. 'Only there's no business like it. No business I know.'

This seemed to satisfy Maroon. 'Yeah ...' he muttered, '... and there's no business more expensive!'

I glanced at his ten thousand dollar walnut desk with four phones – probably one to call his wife, one for his lawyer, and one for each of his two mistresses. I also noticed a silver tray by the window, stacked with bottles of liquor. I licked my lips.

'I'm twenty-five grand over budget on the latest Baby Herman cartoon.'

He paused in front of me.

'You saw the rabbit blowin' his lines?'

I nodded.

'He can't keep his mind on his work. You know why?'

'One too many refrigerators dropped on his head?' I ventured.

Maroon waved this away. 'Nah, he's a Toon. You can drop anything you want on his head. He'll shake it off. But break his heart ...' he sighed '... he goes to pieces just like you or me.'

Something made me wonder whether Maroon was capable of going to pieces, or whether he had a heart.

He opened a desk drawer and pulled out a copy of *Toontown Gossip*, the local trade paper. There was a time when I'd made it my business to keep up with all the goings-on of the Toons but, like Maroon said, when something or someone breaks your heart you just go to pieces. When it came down to Valiant and Valiant, R.K. had hit the nail on the head.

'Read that,' he said, pointing to a front-page headline.

SEEN COOING OVER CALAMARI WITH NOTSONEW SUGAR DADDY WAS JESSICA RABBIT, WIFE OF MAROON CARTOON STAR ROGER RABBIT

I didn't get it.

'What's this got to do with me?' I said.

'You're the private detective, you figure it out.'

This was one job I didn't need. 'Look, I don't have time for this –' I started to say, but Maroon interrupted me.

'Look, Valiant, his wife's poison, but he thinks she's Betty Crocker.'

He came round the desk and drew close to me. If I hadn't smelled a rat before I was smelling it now, and it still wasn't too late to walk out of that office.

'I want you to follow her,' he said confidentially, looking round to make sure he wasn't being overheard. 'Get me a couple of nice juicy pictures . . .' he winked '. . . I can wise the rabbit up with.'

I almost made it to the door. 'Forget it,' I said firmly. 'I don't work Toontown.'

I would never have believed Maroon could be so athletic, he practically sprinted up to pull me back.

'What's wrong with Toontown?' he said, as though offended. 'Every Joe loves Toontown.'

'Then get Joe to do the job, 'cause I ain't goin',' I said, trying to brush him off me. But I hadn't reckoned on his determination.

'Whoa, fella!' he said silkily, leading me back to his desk. 'You don't wanna go to Toontown, you don't have to go to Toontown. Nobody said you had to go to Toontown anyway.'

I suppose I must have still been waiting to hear what the payoff would be. That, or the whiskey I'd drunk – or the thought of that tray by the window – was already addling my brain.

'Have a seat, Valiant,' he said, pushing me down into one of his art deco armchairs.

I sat down. Maybe I was also getting curious.

17

'The rabbit's wife sings at a joint called the Ink and Paint Club.' He returned to his side of the desk. Master and slave. I couldn't help being impressed by his self-assurance. 'Toon revue,' he went on. 'Strictly humans only. OK?'

It didn't sound so bad.

'So what do you think, Valiant?'

I was thinking about the liquor tray.

'Well?' he said.

I glanced at him, then walked round his desk to the liquor tray.

'The job's gonna cost you a hundred bucks...' I began, eyeing the bottles. They sparkled in the sunlight that peeped through the Venetian blinds in slanted stripes.

As I'd expected he got to his feet angrily. Pavlovian reflex, I think they call it.

'... plus expenses.'

'A hundred bucks?' he growled on cue. 'That's ridiculous!'

'So's the job,' I replied, picking up a bottle of Scotch and a shot glass.

Maroon wavered for a moment, then gave in. 'All right, all right. You got your hundred bucks. Have a drink, Eddie,' he added magnanimously.

'I don't mind if I do,' I said.

Outside the window some studio workmen were involved in some kind of tricky operation. I could hear them arguing.

'Careful, Dave!' said one. 'You're gonna drop it.'

'Relax,' came another voice, 'I got it.'

'Careful, Dave.'

'I got it!'

'Dave, you're gonna drop it!'

'I'm not gonna drop it. I'm not gonna –'

'You're dropping it!'

'Watch it.'

While Maroon was getting his check book out of a drawer, I glanced through the blinds. Down below on the lot several workmen were hauling around movie equipment as I'd expected. Two of them, presumably Dave and his pal, were unloading a large crate marked 'Musical Chairs' from the back

18

of a truck.

'Watch it!' said the one who wasn't Dave.

But Dave had had enough. They dropped the crate and a bunch of Toon musical chairs came rolling out, playing 'The Stars and Stripes Forever'. And when I say 'musical chairs', I mean that literally – it's something you have to understand about Toons. It's like someone said, anything that a human being can imagine either probably has existed or will exist. Yeah, and I can tell you where too. In Toontown. Anyway, each of these characters was both a chair and a musical instrument... and a character, if you see what I mean. Think it's spooky? That's Toons for you. A barrel of laughs, but sometimes spooky too. Of course, most of them mean well, I suppose, and are just out for a laugh. But then you get the occasional bad apples. Like the Toon who killed my brother.

Dave and his pal were now arguing over getting the chairs back in the truck.

'Somebody grab the bass.'

'Give me that trombone.'

'We got this one!'

They were rounding them up like chickens.

Suddenly something large, round and grey, with a long trunk and big ears appeared at the window, kind of floating there and blotting out the light.

I let go of the blinds and jumped back.

The elephant squealed.

That was it for me. I hit the floor.

'Kind of jumpy aren't you, Valiant?' said Maroon, coming out from behind his desk to where I was – OK, I'll confess it – hiding.

Maroon checked the blinds.

'It's just Dumbo.'

'I know who it is!' I growled.

'Got him on loan from Disney,' Maroon said matter-of-factly, but I could tell he was boasting. 'Him and half the cast of *Fantasia*.' He opened the blinds and took a jar of nuts from the window sill. 'Best part is ... they work for peanuts.'

Dumbo cooed as Maroon chucked a handful of peanuts out

19

the window. He flew off to catch them, kind of snatching them with his trunk, then flew back to the window again, hovering and cooing.

But Dumbo had had all the peanuts he was getting.

Maroon snapped back the blinds.

'Well, I don't work for peanuts,' I said pointedly.

He held out a check and I took it: fifty bucks.

'Where's the other fifty?'

Maroon put his arm around me – which wasn't exactly my idea of togetherness – and led me back to his desk.

'Let's call the other fifty a carrot to finish the job.'

I looked at him uneasily.

'You been hangin' around rabbits too long,' I said.

3

I stepped out of Maroon's office building wondering what I had got myself into. Still, it was a hundred bucks – which definitely wasn't peanuts back in '47. I was so busy studying the check I almost collided with a cartoon ballerina ostrich on the steps. The Toon patted her feathers and glanced haughtily at me, turning up her nose like I was an affront to her dignity.

'Hmmph!' she remarked and waddled past me.

Toons weren't exactly noted for their dignity.

I tucked the check safely in my pocket and walked past a secretary who was escorting a cartoon toad.

Out on the lot there was the usual kind of activity you'd expect. A couple of studio workmen were moving lighting equipment around and Toon brooms were sweeping up garbage in the soundstage doorway while a (human) musician was playing *The Sorceror's Apprentice* on a saxophone. I double-checked, but it was a human, not a Toon. A cartoon pelican messenger was riding a bicycle out of the soundstage, its neck stretched taut with the effort. I could see a Toon fish peeking out from inside its beak.

Then I bumped into something big and lumbering.

'Oh, excuse me,' said the cartoon hippo as she stepped

round me, crashing into the pelican on his bike.

That's another thing about Toons: they're a bad insurance risk – accident prone, you might say.

The pelican's mail was scattered all over the place, but it wasn't my problem.

A bunch of cartoon cows were all dolled up, preparing for an audition near a sign that read 'Cattle call'. They were mooing and looking flustered, except one who had a kind of contented, grazing look in her big cow eyes. Maybe she'd already slept with the producer.

Out of the corner of my eye I saw the hippo seating herself on a bench next to a studio workman. Next moment, the bench tipped over to the hippo's side, catapulting the workman somewhere off the lot. There was a buzz of consternation and various workmen and Toons tried to help Hippo back on to her feet.

'Oh, oh, oh!' Hippo moaned. 'Oh, please help me. Oh, I'm so embarrassed!'

I almost stumbled on a bunch of gnomes who began tickling my ankles.

'Hey! Hey!' I shouted angrily, kicking them off me.

Out in the street several black dude Toons were greeting each other.

'Hey, ni, Joe,' said a black bear guard at the gate.

'Hey. Eat a bug,' another replied.

'Thanks, Joe.'

The bear hailed a taxi. I thought for a moment of sharing the ride – and then thought better of it. I'd had enough of Toons for one day. Anyway a streetcar had just stopped on the other side of the street, destination Sunset Boulevard, which was where I was headed.

I ran over to the door and pulled out my check to show it to the conductor.

'What do I look like, a bank?' he snarled, and shut the door in my face.

The streetcar started to pull away. I ran behind it and leaped on to the bumper, finding myself seated next to a couple of kids hitching a ride like me.

'Wait for me!' shouted another one chasing after us as the streetcar moved away.

'Come on, Sid!' shouted the kid next to me.

'Hurry up!' yelled his friend.

He was inches away. I grabbed him and pulled him up on to the bumper. He looked at me gratefully. I must admit, I had a lot of time for kids, especially ones who weren't Toons.

'Hey, mister,' said one of them. 'Ain't you got a car?'

I grinned. 'Who needs a car in L.A.? We got the best public transportation system in the world.'

The other kid pulled out a pack of cigarettes and offered them around. Life suddenly didn't seem so bad.

We finally reached the terminal and we climbed off the bumper.

'Thanks for the cigarette, kid,' I said.

'You bet,' he said.

I watched them running off to wherever they called home and made my way to my office. Maybe my mind was on other things. I think I may have seen the sign painters up on the ladders outside the terminal, but I couldn't have been paying any attention.

PACIFIC ELECTRIC: THE WORLD'S FINEST PUBLIC TRANSPORTATION

I knew that sign as well as my own nameplate. So why didn't I notice that the painters were putting up a second sign?

NOW A
Cloverleaf
industry

Would it have changed anything if I had?

The postman was just walking towards my office as I was making for the front door.

'Hi, Eddie?' he said. 'How's it going?'

'OK. What you got for me?'

23

'Oh, the usual bills,' he said, handing me the mail.

I sighed and after he'd walked on I tossed the mail into a nearby trash can. I needed a drink badly. And I needed to see Dolores.

The Terminal Station Bar was one of those run-down joints you could find on every downtown Hollywood street corner after the war. I could have gone somewhere else, but I guess it was the closest thing to home I could think of. Anyway, it was local, convenient, the drinks weren't pricey, and besides, Dolores worked there. Only the word 'Terminal' was still neon-lit, and even that flickered on and off with a loud buzz. Which was appropriate, I guess.

Inside, there was the usual pool crowd. I said hello to a few faces I knew and glanced at a few other faces I didn't know – and didn't want to know. A few drunks were sitting at wooden tables. One of them I recognised. A guy named Earl, an old-timer who worked on the trolleys. He was sleeping it off so soundly that not even the rumble of a passing streetcar, that made the room quake and lights flicker, disturbed his dreams.

I picked up his cap and put it back on his head.

'What's with Earl?' I said, taking a seat at the bar next to a mute cabbie called Augie.

He scribbled out his answer on a notepad and handed it to me.

'Laid off', it read.

I stared at him. 'Laid off?'

'A new outfit bought the Red Car,' said a black soldier who'd followed me in. 'Some big company called Cloverleaf.'

I couldn't believe it. The Red Car had always been around. And so had Earl.

'No kiddin'? They bought the Red Car?'

'Yeah,' said the soldier glumly, 'put the poor guy on two weeks' notice. Cutbacks, they said.'

I had a nasty taste in my mouth. 'Oh, well, Earl.' I picked up a shot glass of whiskey and raised it to the old guy who was snoring soundly. 'Here's to the pencil pushers. May they all get lead poisoning, huh?'

I lifted the glass to my lips but a hand I knew well gripped my wrist and stopped me.

Dolores was one of those dames you thought you could have seen somewhere else, maybe in a movie or in fashion magazine and then you'd look at her closely and think maybe not. It wasn't that she didn't have the looks or class – she had both. But perhaps she was just too nice, underneath the tough act she put on. She was in her thirties, had had a couple of husbands, the first when she was very young. That one ended in a messy divorce. The second had been a pilot, shot down in Europe in the war. She didn't talk about him much but I think it still hurt.

I didn't mind her not talking about that. I didn't mind the tough act. I didn't mind if her make-up was a little too heavy sometimes. Everyone needs some kind of defense. And I didn't mind the way her body went in and out in all the right places. She was a brunette, taller than average – five eight maybe, though if you're my height, any dame over five five is tall. It didn't seem to worry her that she was taller than me. I think she even liked it: gave her some kind of equality, or maybe brought out her mothering instincts. But she did mind my drinking. And there was the small matter of a certain loan ...

'Tomorrow's Friday, Eddie,' she said. 'You know what happens here on Friday?'

'Fish special?' I asked, looking up at her. It was something I liked doing.

She leaned over from behind the bar and pulled the drink out of my hand. In her other hand she was balancing a tray of dirty dishes.

'You know my boss checks the books on Friday and if I don't have that money I gave you back in the till, I'm gonna lose my job.'

'Don't bust a button, Dolores,' I said, looking at her chest as it heaved ever so slightly. 'You've only got one left.'

Then I pulled out my trump card – and held it out to her. She stared at the check in amazement. 'Fifty bucks?'

'Hmm.'

'Where's the rest?' She walked off to serve another

customer.

'Well, it's only a snoop job away,' I called after her. 'Have you got that camera of yours? Mine's in the shop.'

'That wouldn't be the pawn shop by any chance, would it?' Dolores called back, putting the customer's money in the cash register.

'Oh, come on, Dolores. You need the other fifty, I need the camera.'

She sighed, shut the cash register firmly and picked up her camera from the counter.

'Any film in there?'

'Should be,' she replied walking back to hand it to me. 'I haven't had that roll developed since our trip to Catalina.'

I flipped the camera open and checked the lens.

'Sure was a long time ago,' she said wistfully as she arranged donuts on a dish.

I thought back to that vacation with my brother Teddy and Dolores. It had only been last summer but now it seemed like another lifetime.

'Yeah, it was a long time ago. We'll have to do that again sometime.'

She looked at me for a few seconds gravely.

'Yeah, sure, Eddie.'

I tucked the camera in my pocket. Once again a passing streetcar rumbled by, the room quaked and the lights flickered. Dolores stood there with a pile of dishes waiting patiently for the rumbling to stop.

She was a patient woman, Dolores. I think the war must have had something to do with that.

She looked down at the check that was still on the bar counter. 'Is that paper even good?'

'Just check the scrawl,' I said.

She studied the signature. '"R.K. Maroon"? As in Maroon Cartoons?'

'Maroon Cartoons?' came a chuckle from behind me.

It was Angelo. Every bar has its Angelo, exuding a smell of grease and stale sweat and a kind of professional stupidity. I didn't mind the grease and sweat so much as his charm which

26

was none at all. Angelo was constitutionally morose. He only
cheered up when he read about other people's traffic
accidents, which was strange, seeing as how he drove a truck
for a living. He squeezed in beside me at the bar and gave
another stupid chuckle.

'Hey! So who's your client, Mr Detective to the Stars?' He
sniggered. 'Chilly Willy? Or Screwy Squirrel?'

He picked up a hard-boiled egg from the bar.

'What do you want to drink?' Dolores said evenly. She
couldn't afford to get on the wrong side of Angelo. He was a
regular and he always paid his bar bill.

'I'll take a beer, doll.' He turned back to me. His breath
smelt bad. Real bad. 'So what happened, huh? Somebody
kidnap Dinky Doodle?' He chuckled again.

'Cut it out, Angelo,' Dolores muttered.

But Angelo was still warming up. 'Hey, wait a minute. I
know. You're workin' for Little Bo Peep. She's lost her sheep
and you're gonna help her find 'em.' He sniggered. 'Eh?'

Then he chuckled again. It was one chuckle too many for
me. I turned slightly in my seat towards him and kicked his
stool out from under him. He fell forward, his head lolling on
the bar. I stood up and grabbed him from behind.

'Uggh!' he grunted, as I twisted back his arm.

'Get this straight, meatball! I . . . don't . . . work . . . for
Toons!'

'Ugghh!'

I picked up the hard-boiled egg and kind of screwed it into
his greasy mouth, then shoved his face down on to the bar.

As I walked out I could hear Angelo saying plaintively,
through a mouthful of egg, 'So what's his problem?'

'Toon killed his brother,' said Dolores.

'What?' said another drinker.

I didn't hear the rest, but I could imagine how it went:

'Dropped a piano on his head,' Dolores would say.

Which would leave them all speechless.

After all, what can you say after a Toon has dropped a piano
on your brother's head?

4

As Maroon had said, the Ink and Paint Club was strictly human clientele only. Even so, it wasn't exactly the kind of place where the international jet set went. I'd been there once or twice before and each time had regretted going. For one thing I'd yet to find a Toon who could serve a Scotch on the rocks without any funny business. For another, you couldn't conduct any reasonable kind of conversation with cartoons tripping around your feet. I said the clientele was human but the staff was pure cartoon.

The club was at the end of a dark, sleazy alley. I stopped at the dimly lit doorway and knocked with my fist. A panel slid open and the huge, ferocious eyes of a gorilla Toon appeared on the other side.

'Got the password?' Bongo grunted.

'Walt sent me.'

The panel shut and the door opened.

Bongo was built like a brick wall. Ten feet tall, and nearly as wide, the gorilla bouncer had somehow squeezed himself into a tuxedo only fit for a human several feet smaller.

He growled at me.

'Nice monkey suit,' I quipped.

'Wise ass.'

Contrary to popular belief, not all Toons have any sense of humor at all, let alone an undeveloped one.

I walked through a long, dingy passageway, opened the large wooden doors at the far end and stepped inside the nightclub.

To be fair, the interior was as swanky as you could find anywhere in Hollywood. Cartoon penguin waiters waddled up and down, serving drinks to the human patrons, who were in a pretty raucous state at this time of night. On the stage Daffy Duck and Donald Duck were seated at two pianos, playing one of the Hungarian Rhapsodies.

Through the cigar smoke I could see that something was going badly wrong with the duet. Donald, in full tuxedo, was playing at an elegant, polished grand piano while Daffy was playing – if that's what you could call the nonsensical chords he was producing with his elbows – on a rinky-tink upright. The two ducks were in the middle of a heated argument.

'Hey! Hey!' Donald quacked. 'Cut it out!'

Daffy was playing the audience to the hilt. 'Does anybody understand what this duck is saying?' he gagged.

Over at the bar an octopus bartender was babbling to himself and humming to the music mixing several drinks simultaneously with seven of his arms, and lighting the cigarette of a fashionably dressed woman with his one free arm. Her escort was laughing.

'Mmm, most amusing,' she agreed.

The octopus was already serving drinks to another couple, handing the woman a cocktail while taking the money from the man.

Up on the stage the argument was heating up.

'I've worked with a lot of wise quackers,' Daffy Duck hissed, 'but you are des-s-s-picable!'

'Doggone stubborn nitwit!' Donald muttered.

I walked down some stairs into the center of the nightclub. There was a guy sitting with his back to me watching the show and something about his checked suit and balding head looked familiar.

'That did it!' Donald snarled angrily as Daffy clanged an atrocious discord.

'This is the last time I work with someone with a s-s-speech impediment!' Daffy countered.

'Oh, yeah?' Donald stopped playing, reached back and pulled Daffy off his stool. Then he grabbed Daffy and slung him inside the grand piano, slamming the lid so that only Daffy's beak stuck out.

There was a roar of laughter and approval. This was how some people got their kicks. Personally I didn't find it amusing, but then I once had a brother called Teddy.

Donald began playing again, as Daffy climbed out of the piano looking furious.

'This means war!' Daffy screamed.

I pulled out a chair from the table next to the man in the checked suit and was about to sit down when he took out a fountain pen and, to my astonishment, squirted ink on my shirt; then, to my even greater astonishment, he put down the pen and laughed uproariously.

'What?' I said angrily. 'Do you think that's funny?'

'Oh . . .' he was nearly hysterical by now '. . . it's a panic!'

I grabbed him by the collar. 'You won't think it's so funny when I stick that pen up your nose.'

'Now calm down, son, will ya?' he said, pointing to my shirt. 'Look, the stain's gone. It's disappearing ink.'

I stared down at my shirt. Sure enough the ink had disappeared. That's when I remembered who he was.

'No hard feelings, I hope?' He grinned boyishly at me.

I let go of him.

'I'm –' he began.

'I know who you are,' I interrupted. 'Marvin the Gag King, the guy that owns Toontown.'

'Yeah,' he admitted, pleased that I recognised him.

Actually Marvin didn't own Toontown, though he had certainly created it. He'd begun as a magic tricks and gags merchant, going around the fairs, circuses and carnivals at the beginning of the century. He'd branched into the movies before the war when his tricks and characters had started to turn a very big profit. It was well-known that he was still a major shareholder in the Toons. Really he was just a kid, though he was in his sixties at least. So this was Jessica Rabbit's aging Sugar Daddy.

'If it's Marvin's, it's a gasser,' he said proudly. 'Put 'er there, pal.'

He held out his hand and automatically I shook it.

Bzzzzzzzzzzzzzzzzzzzzzzzzzzzzzz.

A mild electric shock went through my hand and up my arm, making my heart beat a few thousand times faster.

I groaned and yanked away my hand.

'The hand buzzer,' he chuckled. 'Still our biggest seller!'

I'd had enough of Marvin and his bag of tricks. I sat down at an adjacent table and Marvin, still laughing, sat back down at his.

A penguin waiter appeared at my side with a menu but by this time I was feeling so disgusted that I threw it down on the table.

'Scotch on the rocks,' I snapped.

Obediently he began to waddle off. Just in time, I called him back.

'And I mean *ice*!'

Up on the stage, Daffy Duck seemed to have temporarily got the upper hand. Donald Duck was nowhere in sight, leaving Daffy a clear run of both pianos, which he was pounding with hands and feet until Donald suddenly emerged from inside the upright, knocking Daffy back into the grand.

Donald now proceeded to play the grand with his hands and the upright with his tail.

'This is hot stuff!' he quacked, stretching himself out to play both pianos with hands, feet and tail.

'Wow!'

Daffy had popped back out of the grand piano with a boxing glove, punching Donald back into the upright and then playing the grand piano with his boxing glove before throwing off the glove and playing with his elbows. Getting bored with this he resorted to playing the piano first with a pair of hammers and then a couple of live chickens.

31

This was more than Donald could stomach. The lid of the upright creaked open to reveal Donald aiming a large cannon at Daffy. He sniggered like a maniac as Daffy brushed back his head feathers and batted his eyelashes.

The next moment I jerked back with a start as there came a deafening bang and the cannonball smashed through the lid of the grand piano. The audience went wild, especially when the grand piano lid fell on top of Daffy, his head poking through the hole.

That's another thing about Toons: whatever props they use – even grand pianos – begin to obey the laws of cartoons. It's unnerving until you get used to it and then it's even more unnerving.

'Who-hoo!' wailed Daffy.

Then before my eyes the two pianos collapsed and giant hooks extended from the wings of the stage. As the audience continued to cheer and Daffy to moan, the hooks grabbed the pianos and the ducks and yanked them off the stage . . . and the curtain came down.

Could I have been the only one in that nightclub to remain completely unamused?

Everyone, including Marvin, but excluding me, was up on his feet yelling and cheering.

'Hey,' he called out to me, 'those ducks are funny. They, they never get to finish the act.'

'Great,' I muttered.

The penguin waiter was hovering.

'Thanks,' I said, taking the Scotch from the tray.

I began to drink it and then felt a hard lump inside the glass. Fearing the worst, I took out the 'ice cube'.

It was a rock.

'Toons,' I sighed, dropping the rock back into the Scotch.

'Cigars, cigarettes?' came a familiar high-pitched voice. 'Eddie Valiant!'

'Betty?'

I looked up to see Betty Boop, looking strangely out of place as a black and white Toon in this full-color world, holding a tray, her big soulful eyes gazing innocently at me.

She was one of the original Toons and, I must admit, I was glad to see her. She'd had a bad deal when Toontown got big, but it was good to know she was still around.

'Long time, no see, Eddie.'

'What are you doing here?'

She fluttered her long black eyelashes. 'Work's been kinda slow since cartoons went to color. But I still got it, Eddie.' She wiggled her hips. 'Boop boop de-doop, boop!'

It was funny, touching, sexy, tragic.

Mainly it was tragic.

'Yeah . . .' I said gently. 'You still got it.'

There was a round of applause as the lights began to dim. At the next table Marvin stood up and began clapping enthusiastically as people began cheering and whistling.

'Oh! Goodie!' Marvin grinned like he was about to eat an ice-cream.

The curtain slowly began to rise and the applause turned to a buzz, a murmur of expectation.

Marvin gave a hoot and pulled out an atomiser to douse himself with cologne.

'What's with him?' I asked Betty.

'Marvin never misses a night when Jessica performs,' she whispered.

'Got a thing for rabbits, huh?'

It looked like I'd be earning my hundred bucks sooner than I'd thought.

The club was almost dark now and then a single spotlight appeared along the runway and centered on the curtain. Some of the male patrons were scrambling for runway seats.

Marvin was winking at me, pointing to the stage as the crowd quietened. Reluctantly I turned to watch. Rabbits don't do much for me. Beside me, Betty Boop adjusted her garter belt.

Picked out by the spotlight, a long slinky leg poked out from behind the curtain and then –

Jessica Rabbit appeared. I couldn't see her face – it was still in darkness – but what I *could* see was that this was no rabbit. It was a Toon, sure, but what a Toon. It was – she was a

33

shimmering, diaphanous vision, a kind of living translucent Venus. Yes, you could say she was more like a goddess than a cartoon. I'd never seen a body like that before. I didn't know bodies could be shaped like that. I had to keep reminding myself that she'd originally been drawn by someone, that no woman really could have breasts like these. They were... astonishing. She was astonishing. Her luminous magenta dress and long silk gloves seemed to have been sprayed on merely to emphasise every contour of her body. I was hypnotised. I looked over at Marvin. He was also hypnotised, like everyone else in that club. I was beginning to understand the old fool. Then she began to sing that old blues number, 'Why Don't You Do Right?'

She moved from behind the curtain then paused, swaying her magnificent breasts and hips.

As she sang she slunk into the center of the spotlight. A round of hoots, catcalls and whistles was released which didn't stop until she had finished. Again she paused and then moved one leg forward towards the edge of the stage.

The spotlight shone on her face. She was the quintessence of a vamp, her luscious red hair falling seductively over one side of her face, adding to the sense of mystery. It was spellbinding.

The curtain began to rise behind her and I could see a little group of cartoon musicians playing the torch-blues song. Jessica began strolling up and down the stage as a couple of Toon crows played an upright bass. She stopped in front of a guy who lay his head down on the stage, and kicked him back into his seat.

I couldn't believe this.

'*She's* married to Roger Rabbit?' I whispered to Betty Boop.

Betty seemed to swoon. 'Yeah. What a lucky girl.' She leaned across to me and closed my mouth. I hadn't realised it had been hanging open.

Jessica began to stroll onto the catwalk. She stopped above a guy who was standing by the runway, drooling up at her. As with the other guy, she pushed him back into his seat.

Next she stopped at Marvin's table and stepped onto it. Marvin was grinning like an idiot. He stood up and took her by the hand. She cuddled him and pinched his cheeks, pulling a scarf out of his breast pocket and rubbing his head playfully. Marvin was now in seventh heaven.

She dropped his scarf on the floor and then, to my excitement and alarm, she moved over towards me, sat on my lap and snuggled up to me, running her fingers inside my collar. She took off my hat and leaned closer to me. She smelled exquisite. At that moment I forgot everything except how I wanted to kiss her – but then, when I tried to, she suddenly shoved my hat into my face.

There's a sucker born every minute.

But she hadn't finished playing with me: she sat on my table while I watched her, dumbstruck. She leaned over and grabbed my necktie, pulling me up even closer to her face . . .

The next moment she had disappeared. I looked up and she was walking back down the runway towards the stage.

She turned and wiggled.

There was uproar: the nightclub erupted in cheers and whistles. As Jessica stepped back on stage, the curtains began to close . . .

The spotlight was now just a sliver along her face and breasts. She gave a final wink and was gone.

As she disappeared behind the curtain and the applause grew even louder, I noticed Marvin getting up and hastily going up the stairs.

I quickly followed him backstage to her dressing-room and was just in time to see Marvin primping himself and holding a bouquet of flowers as he knocked on the door. I hid behind a wall.

'Who is it?' she called out and moments later I heard her open the door.

'Jessica dear, have no fear. Your Marvin is here,' the old fool said as he stepped inside.

The door closed behind them. I crept towards the door and leaned closer to hear – you'd be surprised how much time I've spent in this position but then, that's what gumshoes do – at least, used to do. We didn't have bugs back in 1947 but then on the other hand we had Toons. Even ones who looked like

Jessica Rabbit.

'You sure murdered 'em tonight, baby,' he was crowing. 'I really mean it. My darling, you were superb. You absolutely, truly and honestly fashmolyed that audience.'

I decided to venture peeping through the keyhole, but all I could see was the back of Marvin's fat balding head.

'You killed 'em. You slayed 'em,' he went on.

It was becoming monotonous.

'You belted them. You were terrific.'

I'm sure you've got the drift. I'm sure Jessica must have got it by now. She was good. Very good.

I felt a blow on my back and a dark shadow looming behind me.

I turned. It was Bongo the bouncer, giving me a friendly poke.

'What do you think you're doing, chump?' he growled.

'Who you callin' a chump ... chimp?' I replied.

He grabbed me by the lapels, lifted me off the ground and took me on a tour of the back corridors of the Ink and Paint Club. I've been on better tours with friendlier guides but I'm not complaining. He was only doing his job and I was only doing mine.

Eventually he threw me into a pile of trash cans in the alley. I think the tour had come to an end.

'And don't let me catch your peepin' face round here again,' he growled. 'Got it?' He went back in and slammed the door.

I'd got most of it, though he could have been a little more civilised about it.

I picked myself up, checked for broken bones, and tried out my gorilla walk, scratching under my arms.

'Ooga-booga!'

All I needed was to grow a little more hair and sixty inches.

Further down the alley, beyond the trash cans there was a lighted window. Luck was on my side. It was Jessica's dressing-room. I'd heard the record, now I was going to see the movie. I pulled myself up on to the window sill and tried to look inside. It was just too high for me.

I dropped back to the ground and picked up an old crate. I

36

positioned it below the window and climbed on it, wondering just what I was about to view.

Jessica was sitting at her dressing-table mirror while Marvin was pacing up and down in anticipation.

'Come, my dear Jessica,' I could just about hear him saying. 'Come over here ... I got everything arranged ... right here.'

I took the camera out of my pocket and unfolded it ready. OK, I know it's sleazy, but if it offends you, you're living in the wrong world.

'Oh-h-h, not tonight, Marvin,' Jessica said, a trifle sulkily. 'I have a headache.'

I'd seen this movie before.

'But Jessica, you promised.' Marvin sounded wretched. He really was just a kid.

'Oh, all right,' she relented.

I quickly pointed the camera through the window and began taking shots.

'But this time, take off that hand buzzer,' she added.

'Pattycake,' Marvin began excitedly.

Jessica started to moan in rhythm as he clapped.

I couldn't believe this.

I advanced the film on and took another photo.

'Pattycake.'

'Ooh,' Jessica gasped.

'Pattycake.'

'Marvin!'

'Pattycake.'

'Marvin!'

I took another shot. This was weird stuff, but then what can you expect with Toons involved?

'Pattycake. Pattycake.'

'Marvin!'

'Pattycake!'

'Oh!'

I stopped photographing. It was too much.

'Pattycake!'

'Oh, Marvin!'

'Pattycake! Pattycake! Pattycake!'

'Oh, Marv – Oh, no, Marv!'
I shook my head. This was something out of my league.
'You've gotta be kiddin' me,' I muttered.

5

As Maroon had predicted, Roger Rabbit was heartbroken.

He had climbed on to the window sill of Maroon's office and was violently shaking the blinds.

'Pattycake! Pattycake!' he wept, jumping off the window sill and leaping on to Maroon's desk chair.

'I don't believe it,' he sobbed. 'Pattycake! Pattycake! Is that true?' He banged his head on the desk.

Maroon handed me back the photos.

'Take comfort, son,' he said, his voice ringing with insincerity, though I doubt if Roger noticed. 'You're not the first man whose wife played pattycake on him.'

He took the maroon silk handkerchief from his breast pocket and handed it to Roger, who blew his nose, drenching the handkerchief and creating a puddle in the middle of the desk.

'Oh, I just don't believe it.'

Maroon gingerly took the handkerchief from the rabbit. Behind Roger's back, I held out a trash can and Maroon dropped it inside. I imagine he had a hundred more, all identical, and all with the initials R.K.M. embroidered on them.

'Believe it, kid,' Maroon said.

Roger sobbed and shuddered, looking my way, maybe hoping I was going to say it was all some kind of bad joke. I wish I could have.

'I took the pictures myself,' I confirmed. 'She played pattycake.'

It was time for him to see the evidence. I never liked this part.

'Oh!' Roger Rabbit gasped as I handed him the pictures. In a daze he flipped through them, shaking his floppy ears.

'Not my Jessica,' he wailed. 'Not pattycake. This is impossible! I don't believe it. It can't be!' He flipped through them again, this time so fast that they turned into a cartoon film. 'It just can't be! Jessica's my wife! It's . . .' the animated film was speeding up rapidly now '. . . absolutely impossible!'

He spun around in Maroon's chair, tossing the photographs in the air. 'Jessica's the light of my life . . . the apple of my eye . . .'

His eyes, already red and puffy, grew large and round, like they were about to pop out.

'. . . the cream in my coffee!'

He made a fist like a coffee cup and began stirring it with his finger.

I shrugged. This was getting nowhere. 'Well, you'd better start drinkin' it black,' I said, ''cause Marvin's takin' the cream now.'

I poured myself a Scotch from Maroon's decanter and took a gulp.

Maroon had been gazing through the blinds. He shook his head. 'Hard to believe,' he sighed. 'Marvin's been my friend and neighbor for thirty years. Who would have thought he was a sugar daddy?'

He closed the blinds and turned back to Roger Rabbit.

'Somebody must've made her do it,' the Toon speculated.

Maroon looked at him pityingly, then took the decanter from me and picked up a shot glass.

'Drink this, son. It'll make you feel better.'

He put the shot glass in Roger's hand and poured him a

drink.

The rabbit whimpered a little more, and then, sighing, turned in the chair and gulped down the whiskey.

'Aagh!'

He tossed the glass aside.

I was just about to pour myself a second glass when I noticed something strange happening to the Toon. His cheeks began to swell, his eyes rolled around in his head. He turned purple, and then bright red, making an odd gargling noise in his throat. The next moment he screamed and leaped up in the air. His head seemed to have turned suddenly into a kind of steam whistle and while his body collapsed back on the floor his head was launched like a rocket towards the ceiling. The whistle turned into a piercing shriek. The noise was excruciating and Maroon and I covered our ears as steam billowed out of the demented rabbit's mouth.

At the same time the office seemed to have been taken over by a whirlwind that swept up the papers on Maroon's desk and blew them around. As steam came out of Roger's mouth and ears he was shaking violently and now it was something like a miniature earthquake. Maroon's precious trophies and framed photographs on the wall shattered into pieces. A lamp fell over and bulbs began blowing in the overhead lights. Then there was a further series of explosions as a glass sculpture and even the decanter in my hands shattered.

At last Roger Rabbit's body sprang up to the ceiling to be reunited with his head, which had finally run out of steam, literally. Then he fell face down on to Maroon's desk, picked himself up, looking dazed, and grinned at us.

'Thanks,' he said. 'I needed that.'

So saying, he fell face down on the desk again.

I was drenched in whiskey. 'Look, Mr Maroon,' I muttered, 'I think my work here is finished.'

From the desk came a low moan. After all that, the drink hadn't lifted Roger's spirits one bit.

'How 'bout that carrot you owe me, huh?' I reminded Maroon.

'A deal's a deal,' he replied, taking a check out of his pocket and handing it to me.

'Great. Thanks,' I said, pocketing the check.

We looked over at Roger Rabbit, who was sobbing once more.

'Roger,' Maroon said, trying to choose his words carefully. 'I know all this seems pretty painful now ... but you'll find someone new! Won't he, Mr Valiant?'

'Yeah, sure,' I said, lying through my teeth until I remembered Betty Boop's swoon. 'Good-looking guy like that?' I chuckled encouragingly. 'The dames'll be breakin' his door down.'

'Dames?' Roger Rabbit screamed. 'What dames?'

Then, to my horror, he grabbed me violently by my lapels and shoved me back on to the desk.

'Jessica's the only one for me! You'll see!'

'Damn it,' I grunted as the Toon maintained his attack – he seemed to be trying to suffocate me. 'Get off! Get – Get the –'

'We'll rise above this piddling peccadillo!' he shouted, ignoring me. 'We're gonna be happy again! You got that? Happy!'

He was still holding me down by the lapels, and though he looked just like a skinny rabbit, his strength was almost supernatural.

'Capital H-A-P-P-I!' he spelt out triumphantly.

He finally released me and an instant later shot through the window.

I stared down at Maroon. He stared at me. And we both stared at the perfect Roger-Rabbit-shaped outline that he had left in the shattered blinds.

'Well, at least he took it well,' I said.

The blinds fell off the window, revealing an identically perfect Roger-Rabbit shape in the broken window.

As night fell over the Gag Factory, Roger Rabbit walked wretchedly down the street, sobbing his heart out.

IF IT'S A GAG
IT'S A GASSER

said the sign above the factory. For once in his Toon-life Roger Rabbit had no way of cheering himself up – humor was the life blood of every Toon and he badly needed a transfusion.

He climbed onto some crates outside the factory and pulled out some photographs from his pocket.

'Ohhh!' he sobbed. 'Oh, Jessica!'

He gazed at the wedding photo of himself and Jessica.

'Please tell me it's not true.'

Another photo was of him and Jessica on the beach; a third as they sat in a famous Hollywood restaurant.

Tears welled up once more.

'P-p-p-p-please.'

Roger Rabbit, whose professional career had so depended on making the world tumble around him on the screen had discovered the world tumbling around him inside where it mattered.

And he had no defences: after all, he was only a Toon.

By the time I got back to my office it was past midnight. I switched on the light and almost wished I hadn't when I saw the unmade bed, unwashed dishes, unpaid bills, the trail of empty whiskey bottles. I did the usual things, hanging up my hat, taking off my coat, then walked through to the darkroom and took down the photos I'd just developed and printed.

I tossed aside the photos of Marvin and Jessica – I'd had enough of Pattycake and Roger Rabbit for one night, if not for ever. The next few photographs were of Dolores and me on the beach in Catalina.

I smiled. Maybe it was time for another trip down the coast. It still wasn't too late.

The next photograph took the smile off my face.

Teddy and me were sitting on the beach playing a couple of ukeleles. There was another one with us goofing around on a beach blanket. Well, one thing was for sure: There'd be no more trips for Teddy. I hadn't cried at the funeral. In fact I hadn't cried at all until now. And once the tears came they wouldn't stop. Me and Roger Rabbit, maybe we had something in common after all.

I looked across at Teddy's desk. Everything was still lying

there as he'd left it: his pipe, pens, blotter, magnifying glass, all arranged neatly around his nameplate:

THEODORE J. VALIANT

Cobwebs covered everything.

I glanced at the pages in our old scrapbook. There was the article from the *Los Angeles Chronicle*:

VALIANT AND VALIANT CRACK NEPHEW KIDNAPPING
DONALD'S HUEY, LOUIE AND DEWEY RETURNED
Family Celebrates with Monster Party –
All of Toontown Celebrates

On the opposite page of the scrapbook was our most famous case:

GOOFY CLEARED OF SPY CHARGES
Evidence of Valiant and Valiant decisive

I looked across at the framed photographs that Teddy and I had treasured: the LAPD Police Academy Graduating Class of 1925, with Teddy and me in our police uniforms plus clown make-up. The caption below read:

NEW CLOWNS ON THE BEAT

And then, further back in the past, a sepia photograph of Teddy and me as kids, posing with our father, all three of us in our clown costumes with a banner behind us that read:

RINGLING BROS
and
BARNUM & BAILEY

while the caption above read:

EDDIE & TEDDY ON THE ROAD WITH DAD
[1906]

Finally there was the framed photograph of Teddy and me drinking champagne with Dolores on the steps of our office building:

TWO FLATFOOTS & A FLOOZY GO INTO BUSINESS
[1938]

I went to sleep that night at my desk, cuddling a whiskey bottle and dreaming Teddy, Dolores and I were a trio of Toons, just spreading a little happiness . . .

6

Roger Rabbit was exploding around my office, only this time he had me by the lapels and as we flew towards the window, I was trying to protect my head from smashing into the glass. Too late – there was a shattering sound and I woke up with a start.

Police Lieutenant Santino of the Los Angeles Police Department was flinging empty whiskey bottles into the garbage can. I pulled my head up from the desk – my neck was as stiff as a lump of concrete and my head felt like the rabbit had been jumping up and down on it all night.

'Lieutenant Santino,' I yawned. 'Where'd you come from?'

Santino pulled a face as he looked around at the empty take-out containers that littered my desk and office.

'Gee whiz, Eddie,' he said distastefully, 'if you needed money bad, why didn't you come to me?'

He looked down at the photographs and held them up.

I shrugged. 'So, I took a couple of dirty pictures. So kill me.'

Santino put down the photos and picked up a coffee cup instead, pouring the last few drops from an empty whiskey bottle.

'I already got a stiff on my hands, thank you.'

46

'Huh?'

'Marvin the Gag King. The rabbit killed him last night,' he said almost matter-of-factly.

'What?'

The Toon had been in a terrible state, but was he the type to commit murder? Maybe. Who knows? I thought he was going to kill me the day before, but then again, he wasn't the murderous type. Highly strung, accident-prone, a klutz, yes. A killer... I wasn't sure.

I was still trying to clear my head as Santino drove me to the Gag Factory where Marvin's body had been discovered. It looked like half the LAPD were already up there from the police cars parked outside the factory.

As we got out of the car I froze.

'Now what?' said Santino.

In the distance I could hear the music and sound effects of Toontown and they were bringing back memories I'd rather have forgotten.

'It's just that I haven't been this close to Toontown for a while.'

There was this wall that separated the Gag Factory from Toontown, and if you looked closely you'd see some strange things. If you'd been drinking, you could convince yourself you had a case of the DTs. If you were sober, you might wonder about your sanity. Sometimes there seemed to be a thin line between fun and madness. At that moment there was an explosion behind the Toontown wall. A Toon I recognised as Yosemite Sam went flying into the air.

'Yeo-o-o-o-o-o-o-o-o-o...'

He landed on this side of the wall and bounced around on his butt before coming to rest.

'Ow!' he screeched. 'My biscuits are burnin'.'

He leaped up again and ran around, patting his buttocks, which, sure enough, were smoking.

'Fire in the hatch!' he squealed. 'Ow! Ooh! Eee! Great horny toads, that smarts!'

He sat down in a puddle and extinguished the fire in a burst of steam.

'Aaaah!' he sighed.

I exchanged a glance with Santino, who threw down his cigarette.

'Come on, Eddie,' he said. 'Let's get this over with.'

We turned and walked towards the factory.

'He's with me,' Santino said to the guard, who was looking at me in deep suspicion.

Out on the factory floor two factory workers were already being interrogated by a cop.

'I really didn't see anything,' one was saying nervously. 'I mean, I – I heard this voice, but that's all.'

'Are you sure you work here?' said the cop.

'I'm sure,' the worker replied.

There were the usual groups of police and forensic experts you get at the scene of any murder. Their investigation was obviously centered around a large metal safe sticking out of the floor at an angle in the middle of the factory.

'OK, what about you, fella?' a cop said to another worker.

The worker shifted uneasily. 'I – I didn't see anything. I mean, the worst of it...'

A police photographer was crouched by the safe, winding his camera. Protruding from under the safe on the floor was a chalk outline of Marvin's body, the head outline under the corner of the safe.

'Come on, Lieutenant,' one of the cops said to Santino in a low voice, 'give it to me straight now.'

'Just like a Toon to drop a safe on a guy's head.'

I glared at him and when he saw this he looked down and coughed.

'Sorry, Eddie.' He cleared his throat. 'You better wait here, all right?'

He walked off and I stood there listening to all those familiar phrases I remembered so well from my days at the LAPD. These were the tunes I'd grown up with.

'You get a positive ID on the victim?'

'Just bring him in. We're going to question him.'

'Let's fingerprint him.'

There was a stairway leading up to the factory office and

through the glass door I could make out a figure I'd have recognised anywhere, not just under a spotlight.

They'd already brought Jessica Rabbit in for questioning.

A cop and a forensic expert were rooting through boxes of gags, props and tricks. The forensic guy pulled out a bundle of cartoon dynamite and held it up.

'Hey, Chishold, get a load of this.'

The cop reached into a box marked 'PORTABLE HOLES'. He whisked out a black circle.

'Ever seen one of these?' he grinned.

He threw the black circle at a brick pillar a few yards away. Then he stuck his hand through the circle which had instantly become a hole in the wall.

They laughed.

'Hey, guys,' said another, pulling out a cartoon mallet from a desk.

He pressed a button on the handle. A boxing glove shot out of the mallet. They all instantly ducked out of the way as the glove whizzed past them, knocking over a pile of boxes about twenty feet away. The next moment it sprang back into the mallet. He pointed the mallet in my direction and hit the button again. The glove shot out, narrowly missing me, instead knocking over a pile of 'SINGING SWORD' boxes before springing back into the mallet again.

One of the forensic guys was looking at me curiously.

'Didn't you used to be Eddie Valiant?'

The cops all laughed while I glowered, feeling anger, humiliation and contempt in about equal parts.

'Or did you change your name to Jack Daniels?' he added.

They laughed even louder.

I turned and walked towards the safe: another forensic expert was chipping paint from it.

'What's that?' I asked.

'Paint from the rabbit's glove,' he replied, carefully putting the chips of paint into a forensic bag.

'Mr Valiant?' came a familiar female voice from behind me.

I turned and Jessica Rabbit was standing in front of me. She still had that incredible body but the expression on her face

49

was very different from the one I'd seen when she sat in my lap in the Ink and Paint Club. It could now best be described as livid.

Without saying a word she slapped me hard across the face. I was starting to get used to being attacked by Toons. Still, I guess I had it coming.

'I hope you're very proud of yourself, and those pictures you took.'

She stormed off to the factory door, while the cops and forensic guys stared after her, whistling and chuckling.

I groaned, feeling my face which was still smarting. She could certainly pack a slap.

Behind me two cops were loading Marvin's corpse onto a stretcher. I turned to watch. As they wheeled the stretcher away, one of the cops accidentally backed into a crate labeled 'SQUEAKING SHOES'. He grunted with pain and as the crate toppled over he fell on top of it. The lid burst open and dozens of squeaking cartoon shoes of every size, color and type imaginable escaped.

'Oh, for crying out loud, Mike!' said his colleague angrily as Mike dragged himself up off the crate. 'Hey, we need a little help over here!'

The cops began crawling around on the floor trying to capture the runaway squeaking shoes.

'Hey, somebody grab these loafers!' shouted a cop. The shoes were squeaking around like maniacs, running under the stretcher, kicking the cops or stepping on their toes. A squeaky boot kicked one of the cops carrying the stretcher in the shin. He yowled and let go of the stretcher, which collapsed. Then the nasty little hand buzzer that Marvin had tried on me in the Ink and Paint Club fell out of the stiff's hand, landing beside the chalk outline of the corpse's foot.

The place had gone crazy, of course. Cops were still scurrying around trying to capture the squeaking shoes. Since most of them were down on their knees as the last of the shoes were being rounded up and the lid being put back on the crate, I got down on my knees also. Not to look for shoes or to pray, but to pick up the hand buzzer. Well, it was only logical, wasn't it? Knowing Marvin, he must have buzzed the hand of his killer – there'd be fingerprints – it was right under those cops' noses and they'd missed it. My hand was just closing round it when I felt a sharp pain.

'Oww.'

Bzzzzzzzzzzzzzzzzzzzzzzzzzzzzzz.

A cane struck the back of my hand, setting off the buzzer in my palm. I don't know which hurt more. Reeling from the shock, I looked up from the skull-shaped handle of the cane to its owner: a rail-thin, gaunt giant of a man in a long black cape, black hat, black bow-tie and old fashioned wing collar. From where I was crouching, he looked like some kind of walking angel of death: a skeleton with a chalky-white cadaverous face and long pointed chin. He towered above everyone and though I couldn't see his eyes – he wore dark glasses – I felt pinned down by his stare. I'll admit it, just looking at him at that moment with the buzzer going off in my hand, I was scared as hell. I could have been looking at the Devil himself.

'Is this man removing evidence from the scene of a crime?' he shouted out. His grating voice boomed and echoed around the factory, sending a chill through my bones.

'Uh, no, Judge Doom,' Santino interceded. 'Uh, Valiant here, was just picking it up for you.'

The pressure from the tip of Doom's cane was released. I picked myself up and glared at him. He may have been the Devil himself, but I still had a little trick up my sleeve.

'Weren't you, Eddie?' Santino added encouragingly.

Doom held out his long bony hand.

'Hand it over,' he barked.

I shrugged. 'Sure.'

I shook his hand with the buzzer.

Bzzzzzzzzzzzzzzzzzzzzzzzzzzzzzz.

Judge Doom had gone even more rigid than before: he was shaking violently as I continued squeezing his hand. At last, I relented and Doom pulled his hand free, though he was still quivering a little.

'His number one seller,' I explained.

Doom looked down at the buzzer and then grinned at me horribly.

'I see working for a Toon has rubbed off on you.'

'I wasn't workin' for a Toon,' I reacted angrily. 'I was workin' for R.K. Maroon.'

He nodded. 'We talked to Mr Maroon. He told us the rabbit became quite agitated when you showed him the pictures. The rabbit said one way or another he and his wife were going to be happy. Is that true?'

'Hey, pal,' I snapped, 'do I look like a stenographer?'

The walking corpse was getting my back up.

'Shut your yap, Eddie,' Santino hissed at me. 'The man's a judge.'

Doom grinned. 'That's all right, Lieutenant. From the smell of him, I'd say it was the booze talking. No matter, the rabbit won't get far. My men will find him.'

At that moment there was a screech of tires and the smell of gasoline: the doors burst open and an old crock I recognised as the Toon Squad paddy wagon tore through the factory: cops fled in all directions as it roared past us and skidded into a pile of 'ITCHING POWDER' boxes, which toppled over.

'Weasels!' I muttered.

Doom looked on proudly at his 'men': four sinister – not to say vicious-looking – Toon weasels whose names, I quickly found out, were Smart Ass (the driver and, naturally, the leader of the Toon Squad), Psycho, Stupid and Wheezy.

'Yes,' Doom said suavely, 'I find they have a special gift for the work.'

'All right, ya mugs, fall out,' said Smart Ass, climbing out of the front of the paddy wagon.

The other weasels piled out, laughed shrilly.

'Did you find the rabbit?' Doom snapped at them.

'Don't worry, Judge,' piped up Smart Ass. 'We've got deformants all over the city. We'll find him.'

What was going on here? Los Angeles law enforcement was being taken over by a bunch of illiterate, moronic Toon weasels controlled by a corpse. Things were looking bad.

The other weasels coughed and sniggered behind their leader.

Doom stepped back and peered down at me. '*You* wouldn't have any idea where the rabbit might be, Mr Valiant?'

'Have you tried Walla Walla?' I ventured. 'Cucamonga? I hear Kokomo's very nice this time of the year.'

The irony was lost on Doom. He frowned and advanced on me with the look of murder on his chalky, chiselled features.

'I'm surprised you're not more co-operative, Mr Valiant. A human has been murdered by a Toon. Don't you appreciate the magnitude of that?'

I appreciated it all right. I didn't need this sneering skeleton to remind me of my brother's death.

What was bothering me was, why was Doom so interested in pinning the murder on the rabbit? What was his angle?

I soon had my answer – or thought I had. The Judge looked down in disgust and I saw that a single squeaking shoe had cuddled up to his feet. That's the trouble with Toons, they've got no sense of who their friends are – and who aren't. Like a surgeon about to perform a gruesome operation, Doom tucked his cane under his arm and took out a black rubber glove.

'Since I've had Toontown under my jurisdiction,' he barked, 'my goal has been to rein in the insanity, and the only way to do that is to make Toons respect the law.'

He slid the rubber glove up his hand and arm with a loud snap, then reached down for the squeaking shoe. From where I was standing I could see his thin, bloodless lips curling up with a look of malicious relish.

The shoe squeaked a bit more, trying to run away, but Doom's gloved hand reached down and grabbed it. He held it dangling in front of his face with sadistic pleasure as the shoe squeaked in terror. Then, followed by his weasels, he carried it over to the paddy wagon.

'How did that gargoyle get to be a judge?' I whispered to Santino as Greasy opened the back door of the paddy wagon. Inside was a large barrel labelled 'TURPENTINE'.

'He spread a bunch of simoleons around Toontown a couple years back,' Santino muttered. 'Bought the election.'

I pointed at the barrel. 'What's that?'

Doom was pulling the lid off the barrel and suddenly a revolting stench filled the factory. Inside the barrel was an evil-looking yellowish-green mixture, boiling and bubbling like the contents of a witch's cauldron.

'Remember how we always thought there wasn't a way to kill a Toon?' Santino hissed.

'Yeah.'

'Well, Doom found a way. Turpentine, acetone, benzene. He calls it "The Dip".'

'I'll catch the rabbit, Mr Valiant,' Doom announced, dangling the terror-stricken squeaking shoe over the barrel. 'Then I'll try him, convict him . . . and execute him.'

The shoe was now squealing and screaming as Doom lowered it slowly towards The Dip.

Psycho the weasel laughed hysterically.

The shoe touched the top of the bubbling mixture. Billows of smoke and noxious fumes began to rise from the barrel as the shoe started to melt.

Doom grinned and dunked the shoe completely into The Dip.

OK, it was only a Toon – and just a shoe at that – but I was horrified. What I was seeing was nothing like pest control, or state execution, not even your average murder – it was an act of pure evil and I think it was the ghastly smile of satisfaction on Doom's face as the shoe dissolved, still squealing pitifully, that got to me.

Santino turned his head away.

'Geez!' I gasped.

Psycho shrieked with laughter once more as Doom's face emerged from the smoke; then he lifted his gloved hand from The Dip: it dripped with the melted remains of the squeaking shoe.

'That's one dead shoe, eh, boss?' Greasy laughed.

That's one mad judge, I thought.

'They're not kid gloves, Mr Valiant,' said Doom, approaching me menacingly. 'But this is how we handle things down in Toontown.'

Then a chill went through me as he added, almost under his breath:

'I'd think you, of all people, would appreciate that.'

7

I was still trying to figure out what Doom had meant by his remark about me of all people being able to appreciate his gruesome methods of eliminating Toons as I climbed the steps to my office. If he knew about Teddy's death, why hadn't he come right out and mentioned it? Was it possible that he knew the Toon who had murdered him? Was he giving me a warning of some kind?

But the sight that greeted me at the top of the stairs made me forget all about Doom and think more about nice things like gorgeous blondes who are in deep trouble and need a guy like Eddie Valiant to help them out and then they're so grateful that they'd do anything to show their thanks. The blonde had a shapely ass, which was what I noticed first because it was pointed straight at me as she bent over a baby carriage. I checked out her legs, which is one of my hobbies, especially when they go on for ever like these did.

She turned her head and glanced at me, then straightened up and took out a cigarette lighter. I waited for the usual routine. Oh, wouldn't you know it? My lighter's not working, have you got one? But I was wrong. It worked perfectly, first time. Then, to my dismay and horror, she bent down with the flame into the baby carriage. What was she? Some kind of maniac?

I started to run towards her. 'Hey!' I shouted. 'Hey, hey, hey!'

I reached her seconds later and pulled her away from the carriage. 'Hey! Hey, wait a minute!'

She stepped aside and I looked down in astonishment.

It was Baby Herman, Roger Rabbit's playmate. He was smoking a cigar and looking very angry. He blew smoke in my face.

'I've been trying to make him quit,' said the blonde sullenly, 'but he just won't listen to me.'

Baby Herman poked his pudgy arm out of the carriage and flicked cigar ash on the floor.

'What do you know, you dumb broad?' he growled. 'You got the IQ of a rattle.' He stared at me. 'You Valiant?'

'Yeah.'

'I wanna talk to you about Marvin's murder.' He leaned over and beckoned the blonde. 'Hey, pssst . . . Doll! Why don't you run downstairs and get me a racin' form!'

Then to my shock this hard-boiled three-year-old slapped her on the rear.

She squealed. 'OK, OK, I'm goin'!'

He peered round to view the movements of her chassis as she walked off. Me too.

I turned back to him.

'Lady's man, huh?' I said.

He slipped the cigar back in his mouth and looked disgusted. 'My problem is, I got a fifty-year-old lust and a three-year-old dinkie.' He pointed at his groin.

I glanced down at him sympathetically. 'Yeah, must be tough.'

'Look, Valiant,' said the baby, getting down to business. 'The rabbit didn't kill Marvin. He's not a murderer. I should know. He's a dear friend of mine. I tell ya, Valiant, the whole thing stinks like yesterday's diapers. Look at this.'

He pulled a newspaper out of his carriage and handed it to me. I opened it and read the front-page headlines.

'The papers said Marvin left no will. That's a load of succotash! Every Toon knows Marvin had a will.' He gestured with his pudgy hands. 'He promised to leave Toontown to us Toons. That will is the reason he got bumped off.'

'Has anybody ever seen this will?' I asked sceptically.

He poked his head out of the carriage. 'Uh, no, but he gave us his solemn oath.'

Another time-wasting Toon. I folded the paper and began to walk past him. 'If you believe that that joker could do anything solemn, the gag's on you, pal.' I unlocked the carriage wheels and spun the carriage round to face the stairs, then walked on towards my office.

'I just figured you were the one who got my pal in trouble . . .' Baby Herman called after me.

I was in the middle of unlocking my door. I stopped and turned back to face the little monster.

'. . . you might wanna help get him out,' he finished.

He flicked more cigar ash on the floor and looked up at me as I walked back to the carriage.

'I can pay you,' he added hopefully.

That did it. 'Save your money for a pair of elevator shoes!' I snapped, giving the carriage a shove.

'Wait . . .' Baby Herman shouted as I returned to the door of my office.

I watched as the carriage rolled down the corridor, crashing into the blonde as she came up the stairs with the racing form.

'No! Valiant, don't!' Baby cried and the blonde screamed.

The cigar slipped out of his mouth and the carriage mowed down the blonde.

'Aah, my stogie!' Baby Herman moaned.

I could see him leaning over the side of the carriage to find his cigar. Then he looked up and began bawling.

I left it to the blonde, who was lying splayed out behind the carriage, to deal with Baby's fully fledged temper tantrum.

TOON KILLS MAN
MARVIN THE GAG KING MURDERED
AT THE HANDS OF A JEALOUS RABBIT

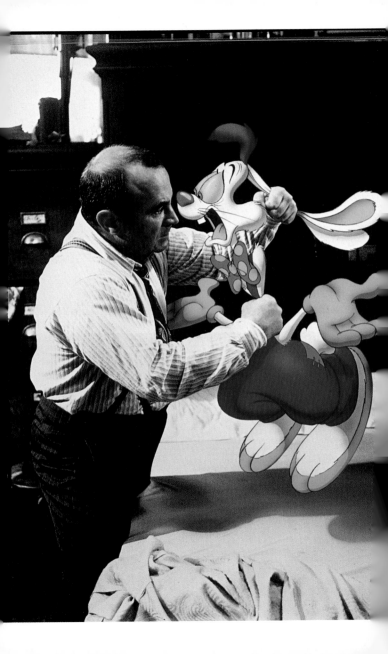

Below the main headline was a nasty little piece about my part in the business. I unfolded the paper on my desk and read, under the pictures of Roger Rabbit on one side, and Jessica playing pattycake with Marvin on the other:

GAG KING LEAVES NO WILL
Snoop Valiant Fans Flames of Jealousy

It wasn't my fault the rabbit had got himself in trouble, I thought. But I guess my conscience was pricking me a little, though why I can't say. All I had done was take a couple of lousy pictures.

I downed a glass of whiskey and set the empty glass on top of the newspaper.

I leaned over to take off my shoes and then something made me stop. Through the empty glass the newspaper picture of Marvin and Jessica was slightly magnified and I could just make out, sticking out of Marvin's pocket, some kind of document. I wasn't sure – it might have been my imagination – but I thought I could see some writing on it.

I pulled out the briefcase from my desk drawer, opened it and took out my magnifying glass. I was about to inspect the newspaper picture again, but then remembered I had the originals. I tossed the paper aside and pulled out one of the photos of Jessica and Marvin. Then I examined it through the magnifier.

LAST WILL AND TESTAMENT

There it was, as plain as anything.
'The Baby was right!' I muttered.

I thought about this for a moment. After all, what had I to gain from getting involved in it now? I'd had enough of helping Toons – and I didn't fancy getting mixed up with anything in which Judge Doom was involved. So Marvin was carrying his will. That didn't necessarily mean anything except that, as was often the case in my experience, the Press had got it wrong.

Besides, I badly needed some sleep.

'The hell with it!'

I yawned, stretched, rubbing my hands down my buttocks, still sore from Bongo's farewell drop. Then I walked over to what visitors fondly imagined was a wall of filing cabinets stuffed full of Valiant & Valiant case files. I pulled down on a lever and the filing cabinets dutifully broke ranks with the rest of the wall and collapsed into a bed. I sat down at the edge of the bed and undressed, then climbed in bed, lying on my back and closing my eyes. It felt good to relax and unwind and I rolled over to my side and stretched my legs . . .

There was something in my bed.

Something . . . or someone.

I opened my eyes and screamed.

It was something like a clown with pink floppy ears, a red shiny nose and a crazed look in its dopey eyes. And a bow-tie.

We screamed at each other and jumped out of bed.

I landed on the floor on my side. He landed on the dresser.

'How the hell did you get in here?' I demanded angrily.

'Through the mail slot,' Roger Rabbit said apologetically. 'I thought it would be best if I waited inside, seeing's how I'm wanted for murder!'

'No kiddin'! Just talking to you could get me a rap for aiding and abetting.'

He cringed.

'Wait a minute,' I went on, struck by a thought. 'Anybody know you're here?'

'Nobody!' he assured me confidently. 'Not a soul! Except, uh . . .'

'Who?'

'Well, you see . . .' He leapt up on my bed and waved his arms about. '. . . I didn't know where your office was, so I asked the newsboy. He didn't know, so I asked the fireman, the greengrocer, the butcher, the baker. They didn't know! But the liquor store guy . . . *he* knew!'

He grinned, pleased with his little joke.

I couldn't see anything funny about it. I grabbed him, kicking and struggling and flailing his stringy, loopy arms.

'In other words,' I shouted, 'the whole damn town knows you're here! Come on! Get out of here!' – while that stupid rabbit was needling me with his wheedling, 'Hey! All right, Eddie, take it easy, willya? Please, Eddie!'

I opened the door and tried to throw him outside but the rabbit grabbed hold of the door-frame and resisted, stretching himself like a piece of chewing gum.

'Get out!' I yelled. 'Come on, out! Get out!'

'Don't throw me out! You're makin' a big mistake!'

He had wedged himself tightly into the door and it was impossible to budge him. I tried pushing.

'Get your hands off that door, willya!' I grunted.

'I didn't kill anybody! I swear!'

I turned around and shoved my back against him.

'This whole thing's a set-up. A scam!'

I held on to his pant legs and tried to pull him back out of the doorway. Then I stepped back and stretched his legs but he seemed to be infinitely elastic.

'Eddie,' he was pleading, 'I could never hurt anybody! Ow!'

'Geez, let go of that door, willya?'

I tugged him violently but he just wouldn't budge. Then I stepped back and stretched his legs once more, this time across the entire length of the office.

'My whole purpose in life is to m-make peopl-l-le . . .'

At last his legs seemed to have stretched to their limit, and I kept on pulling.

'Let go!' I groaned.

'. . . laugh!'

At last, obligingly, he let go of the door and shot back across the office like a bullet, knocking me to the floor.

'OK, OK! Sure, I admit it!' he cried, leaping on the bed. 'I got a little steamed when you showed me those pictures of Jessica. So I rushed over to the Ink and Paint Club . . .'

I dragged myself up from the floor and made a lunge for him but he leaped out of the way and I tumbled over the other side of the bed. The rabbit landed back on the bed and carried on imperviously:

'But she wasn't in her dressing-room, so I wrote her a love

61

letter.'

I sat up and leaned over the edge of the bed, wondering if I'd heard him right.

'Wait a minute. You're telling me . . . that in a fit of jealousy, you wrote your wife a love letter?'

'That's right. I know it. She was just an innocent victim of circumstance.'

'I suppose you used the old lipstick on the mirror routine, huh?'

'Lipstick, yes. Mirror, no. I found a nice clean piece of paper.' He pulled out a large sheet of paper, unfolded it dramatically and began to read it like he was up on the screen. '"Dear Jessica. How do I love thee? Let me count the ways."'

He began jumping up and down on the bed excitedly while I stood up.

'"One, one thousand. Two, one thousand. Three, one thousand. Four, one thousand. Five –"'

'Why didn't you just leave the letter there?' I interrupted this dreary monologue.

He leaped off the bed after me. 'Obviously, a poem of this power and sensitivity must –'

Wherever I walked the rabbit seemed to get under my feet. He wasn't just irritating – he was maddening.

'Will you –' I tried to get round him and finally yanked him up by his ears and slung him out of the way. He screamed but then carried on intrepidly:

'– be read in person, so I went home to wait for her.'

I retreated behind my desk.

'But the weasels were waiting for me, so . . . so I ran.'

'So why come to me? I'm the guy that took the pictures of your wife!'

He was looking through the scrapbooks on Teddy's desk.

'Yeah, and you're also the guy that helped all these Toons.'

I poured myself a Scotch and took a sip.

'Everybody knows when a Toon's in trouble, there's only one place to go – Valiant and Valiant.'

I frowned. 'Not anymore.'

The rabbit was starting to sit down and for me at that moment it was the last straw.

'Get out of that chair!' I stormed angrily, getting up from my seat. 'That's my brother's chair.'

'Yeah, where *is* your brother, anyway?' he said with a look of accusation. He examined one of the framed photographs. 'He looks like a very sensitive and ... *sober* fellow.'

I was sure the rabbit was needling me just for the hell of it. I slammed down the whiskey glass angrily and picked up the phone.

'That's it! I'm callin' the cops.' I began to dial.

Roger affected a look of heroic martyrdom. 'Go ahead! Call the cops!'

He put a hand melodramatically to his brow and walked towards the closet door.

'I came here for help and what do you do? You turn me in! No,' he held up a hand, 'don't feel guilty about me.' He opened the closet door and slumped against it tragically.

I sat transfixed, with the telephone receiver in mid air, staring at the rabbit and wondering if he could be for real. It was the most extraordinarily ridiculous performance I'd seen since ... since his performance the previous day in Maroon's office.

'So long!' he sobbed, 'and ... thanks for nothin'!'

He disappeared inside the closet and slammed the door behind him. I could hear the sound of books falling on top of him from the closet shelf.

'That's the closet ... stupe!' I bawled.

I hung up the phone, walked over to the closet, flipped on the switch and opened the door. There was my trenchcoat and hat hanging inside but I couldn't see the rabbit. I stepped inside to look for him – and then my heart jumped as a face like that of a cop popped out of my trenchcoat.

'Eddie Valiant,' he grabbed my wrist and slapped a handcuff on it. 'You're under arrest!'

An instant later the policeman's face turned back into Roger Rabbit's. He wiggled his lips.

'Get out of there!' I yelled in fury, yanking him out of the trenchcoat.

'Hey!'

I threw him on the bed, but he dragged my arm with him. The rabbit had handcuffed my wrist to his.

'Idiot!' I shouted. 'I got no keys for these cuffs!'

'Huh?'

At the same movement we both heard the sound of a distant siren. The rabbit froze, shuddered, then panicked, leaping over to the window and dragging me with him. Through the blinds I saw the Toon Squad paddy wagon pulling over to the curb in the street below, banging into a parked car. Then the weasels climbed out, stopping the traffic as cars screeched to a halt on either side.

'Come on, get the lead out!' snapped Smart Ass. 'Move it, would ya! Move it!'

Roger screamed and leapt off the window sill, his eyes bulging in terror.

'Come on, Roger!' I groaned. 'Owww, Roger!'

'It's the Toon Patrol!' he whimpered, diving to the floor and yanking me down and dragging me under the bed. I felt a huge great weight descending on me.

'Oooooh!' he was moaning.

Suddenly my bed sprang back up into the wall and I stared up at the rabbit who was crouched on top of me. He jumped off and ran over to Teddy's desk, pulling me with him.

'Hide me, Eddie!' he begged. 'P-p-p-please!'

He opened a drawer and leapt inside, trapping my wrist in the edge of the drawer.

'Ughhh!' I screamed.

His head popped out of the drawer. 'Remember, you never saw me.'

'Get out of here!' I growled.

He pulled on my arm and his head disappeared back into the drawer. But I wasn't going to have my life ruled by a rabbit or a set of cuffs. I yanked him out of the drawer and plopped him on top of Teddy's desk.

He was trembling and quivering as he pleaded with me.

'Don't let 'em . . . find me! Come on, Eddie. You're my only hope.'

I looked across to the office door. The elongated shadows of four weasels appeared in the glass. Roger's ears shot straight up into the air in abject terror.

'Open up in the name of the law,' came Smart Ass's high-pitched weasel voice.

'Open up, Valiant, we know you're in there!' Greasy chimed in. The rabbit was in a blue funk. 'P-p-p-please, Eddie. You know there's no justice for Toons. If the weasels get their hands on me, I'm as good as dipped.'

'Don't make us play rough, Valiant. We just want the rabbit,' shouted Smart Ass.

'What are we gonna do, Eddie? What are we gonna do?' Roger wailed.

I raised an eyebrow. 'What's all this "we" stuff? You heard 'em. They just want the rabbit.'

The Toon Squad began blasting bullets through the wood all around the doorknob. It wasn't an expensive door, but I happened to be fond of it.

And when the knob fell off the door I decided that enough was enough.

8

I heard the door creak open, and Wheezy grunting and wheezing as the weasels stepped inside the office.

'Looks like they gave us the slip, boss,' came a slimy voice. It must have been Greasy.

'Nah. Valiant's got him stashed somewhere.' That was Smart Ass.

I was standing at the sink, humming as I washed my clothes when he sneaked his head round the partition wall of the kitchen area of the office.

'Hold it right there!' he snapped, pointing his revolver at me. He beckoned to the other weasels to join him.

'Hello boys,' I said, friendly. 'I didn't hear you come in.'

Smart Ass slid a chair over to the sink. 'OK, wise guy,' he said, climbing up on the chair and pointing the revolver at my head, 'where's the rabbit?'

I shrugged. 'Haven't seen him.'

He sniffed at my shirt and pointed down into the sink.

'What's in there?' He sniffed again.

I pulled out a soaking sock from the sink and hung it up to dry. 'My lingerie.'

The weasel narrowed his eyes and nodded. 'I see, Valiant.'

He climbed off the chair and walked out of the kitchen. A split second later, Roger Rabbit popped up out of the sink water, spluttering and gasping. Just then Smart Ass sneaked another look round the partition. I plunged the rabbit back under the water just in time.

He rejoined the other weasels in the office. 'Search the place, boys. And leave no stone unturned.'

I heard them going through my desk drawers and then Smart Ass appeared once more in the kitchen.

'Look, Valiant,' he said. 'We got a reliable tip-off the rabbit was here.' Again he leaped up onto the chair and pointed his revolver at my head. 'And it was corrugated by several others.'

He poked the gun barrel in my cheek so I was forced to lean back.

'So cut the bullshtick!' he snapped.

I wasn't going to be threatened by a Toon weasel. I pulled out a bar of soap from the water.

'You keep talkin' like that and I'm gonna have to wash your mouth out!' I snarled, and shoved it in his mouth.

He fell back off the chair with the soap in his mouth, crashing into a pile of boxes on the floor, and rolling out of the kitchen just as the rabbit popped back out of the water, gasping and spluttering.

Soap bubbles began to float out from the office where the weasels were laughing hysterically at their boss. I could hear him making a desperate attempt to maintain his command over them.

'Stop that laughing . . . a-chooo!'

He sneezed and spat out the soap.

This set them off on a further round of laughing.

'You know what happens when you can't stop laughing!' he hissed.

I peered through the doorway and could see him pick up the sink plunger and hit Greasy and Psycho over the head with it. Then he threw the plunger at Stupid, who had collapsed against a filing cabinet in hysterics. The plunger clamped on to Stupid's face, knocking him back against the cabinet.

'One of these days you're gonna *die* laughing,' Smart Ass

shouted and walked back into the kitchen, kicking a box out of his way.

Yet again he climbed up on the chair and pointed the revolver at me.

'As for you, Valiant,' he hissed, 'step out of line and we'll hang you and your laundry out to dry.'

He chuckled at his joke, splashed water in my face, jumped off the chair and scampered out of the kitchen.

'Come on boys,' he barked. 'Let's am-scray.'

The door slammed and their weasel footsteps receded down the stairs.

For the final time Roger Rabbit popped out of the sink, spewing a stream of water in my face.

'They're gone,' I announced, wiping my face with a towel.

'Jeepers, Eddie, that was swell,' said the rabbit, grabbing the towel from me to wipe himself. 'You saved my life! How can I ever repay ya?'

Then he leaped into my arms and planted a revolting kiss on my mouth.

'Mmmmmm!'

'Uggggh!' I grunted and spat into the sink. 'For starters, don't ever kiss me again.'

'OK,' he said obediently. 'Anything else?'

'Yeah,' I said. 'I need a drink.'

Imagine the picture, I'm wearing my trenchcoat and the rabbit's hidden inside, but he keeps popping his head out to make some wisecrack or other. But what else could I do? I needed help, and Dolores was the only one I could trust.

So I laid down the law. No wisecracks. No popping his head out. If he wanted to come on the outing he was going to have to be a good little rabbit. I must admit, there were moments when I could have taken a leaf out of the judge's book and chucked Roger in The Dip myself.

'Come on, Eddie, just let's go!' he kept saying.

'Get . . . down,' I grunted, shoving him deep down in my trenchcoat as I walked in the bar.

'So tell me, Eddie,' said Dolores staring at the bulge around my groin, 'is that a rabbit in your pocket or are you just happy to see me?'

I took her by the arm and led her away from the bar. 'Cut the comedy, Dolores. I've had a very hard day.'

We moved into a little alcove where we could be alone – just me and Dolores and, of course, the rabbit – and she pulled the curtain closed behind us.

'I got to get out of these cuffs.'

'Oh, swell,' she said. So what did she expect? A smooch with Roger?

The rabbit popped his head out of my coat as Dolores opened a secret door in the wall and led us through to a store room. I bumped my head on a hanging lamp as she shut the door.

'Boy, what is this? Some kind of a secret room?'

I took off the trenchcoat and Dolores turned on the light. 'It's the Rot Gut Room,' she said. 'Holdover from Prohibition.'

'Oh, I get it. A speakeasy,' said the rabbit. 'A gin mill. A hooch parlor.'

'Tools are up here, Eddie.' She pointed towards a shelf on the wall.

I was holding the rabbit by the ears – that way I kept him under control.

'Look at this!' He scrambled around in mid-air before dragging me over to a hole in the wall. I fell down on a bed, and Dolores tumbled down with me as the rabbit peeked through the hole.

'It's a spy hole.'

Dolores gave me a look that said, is he always like this? and I replied with a look that said, you ain't seen nothin' yet.

'Jeepers, Eddie. This'll be a great place to hide.'

The bar was on the other side of the wall and Roger's eyes, bulging through the hole, managed to knock down a beer bottle. He immediately backed away from the hole.

'Crazy Toon!' I muttered, taking down the toolbox from the shelf and carrying the rabbit away from the wall, bumping my head on the lamp again.

'Oooh, watch your head,' said the rabbit helpfully.

I could have strangled him, but then again, knowing how elastic he was, I probably couldn't. I opened the toolbox as Dolores closed a panel over the hole.

'I thought you said you'd never take on another Toon case,' she said. 'What'd you have, a change of heart?'

I shook my head grimly and took a saw out of the box. 'Nothin's changed. Somebody's made a patsy out of me and I'm gonna find out why!'

I set Roger Rabbit down on the floor and sat down on the bed, then spread the handcuff chain across a crate and started sawing it as the rabbit began squirming around.

'Hold still, will ya!' I snapped.

'Does this help?' He slipped his wrist out of the handcuff and stepped around to the other side of the crate.

'Thanks,' I said, and went on sawing.

It suddenly clicked.

I stopped sawing and swung round. The rabbit quickly slipped his wrist back into the handcuff.

'Do you mean to tell me that you could have taken your hand out of that cuff at any time?'

The rabbit looked shocked. 'No, not any time. Only when it was funny!'

'Get outta here!' I thundered.

He slipped his hand out of the handcuff again, leaped over the counter and twirled on a stool.

'Come on, Eddie!' he wheedled. 'Where's your sense of humor?'

Dolores whistled. 'Is he always this funny or only on days when he's wanted for murder?'

'Listen, my philosophy is this: if you don't have a sense of humor, you're better off dead.'

I put down the saw and took a rolled-up photograph out of my trenchcoat pocket. 'You may just get your wish unless I can figure out what happened to this.'

I threw them the blow-up I'd made of the will in Marvin's pocket.

Dolores caught it and the Toon leaned over the counter to

look at it.

'What is it, Eddie?'

'Just look at it.'

He stared. 'It's Marvin's will.'

'Yeah.' I carried on sawing the handcuffs. 'And I think Maroon played the part of sound mind and your wife the sound body.'

'Why, I resent that innuendo!' said the Rabbit, waving a hammer around until Dolores took it away from him and replaced it in the toolbox.

'What's the scheme, Eddie?' she asked me.

'I don't think they got to the will,' I said, panting from the effort of sawing.

The light was swinging from side to side: the rabbit was dangling from it, but I decided to let him have his fun.

'But how do you know?' said Dolores.

'Because they were still lookin' for it *after* they killed him.'

She sat on the bed beside me and held the handcuffs steady for me.

'Anything I can do?' she asked.

'Maybe you could go downtown and check the probate.'

'Yeah,' said Roger Rabbit, standing on the counter holding a wrench, 'check the probate. Why, my Uncle Thumper had a problem with his probate, and he had to take these big pills and drink lots of water.'

'Not prostate, you idiot!' I said. 'Probate!'

'Let me get this straight,' the rabbit said, actually being serious for once. 'You think that my boss, R.K. Maroon, dropped a safe on Marvin's head . . . so that he could get his hands on Toontown?'

The saw had finally cut through the handcuffs and I removed them, standing up and grabbing my trenchcoat. 'Yep. That's my hunch.' I turned to Dolores. 'Can he stay here for a couple of days?'

She eyed the rabbit dubiously. 'He's not gonna do anything crazy, is he?'

At that moment he was running a large metal file back and forth through his ears and making ludicrous faces.

I made for the door.

'Where are you going?' said Dolores.

'Back to the office.'

She looked back in alarm at Roger Rabbit who opened his mouth – but before he could make another wisecrack I was gone.

9

She still looked like a million dollars – and her timing was perfect. She arrived at my office as I was coming out of the john, holding a pair of pants up around my waist and with a necktie around my bare chest.

She wiggled through into my inner office, took a small mirror from her bag and began applying crimson lipstick.

'You've got the wrong idea about me, Mr Valiant.'

I thought I had a pretty good idea about her. I remembered how it felt when she sat on my lap in the Ink and Paint Club, but then I remembered how it felt when she'd slapped me on the cheek in the Gag Factory and on balance I decided she wasn't the type you could afford to play pattycake with or you might just end up dead like poor old Marvin.

'I'm a pawn in this, just like Roger,' she sighed. 'Can you help me find him? Just name your price . . . and I'll pay it.'

'Yeah, I bet you would. You've got to have the rabbit to make the scam work.'

She put down the mirror and turned to me. The protesting, innocent wife. I'd seen it all before. 'No, no, I love my husband. You've got me all wrong.'

She walked past me, swaying her hips. 'You don't know

73

how hard it is being a woman... looking the way I do.' She adopted the same seductive pose she'd used at the end of her act in the club, looking back at me.

'Yeah, well...' my throat had suddenly gone dry and I was feeling weak at the knees. '... you don't know how hard it is being a man... looking at a woman looking the way you do.'

She held the pose, glancing back at me. 'I'm not bad,' she explained. 'I'm just drawn that way.'

I walked over to the couch, picked up a shirt and put it on. 'Weren't you the one I caught playing pattycake with old Marvin?'

Her breasts were swaying back and forth, but, God's my witness, the rest of her wasn't moving.

'You didn't catch me, Mr Valiant. You were set up to take those pictures.'

'What are you talkin' about?'

'Maroon wanted to blackmail Marvin. I didn't want to have anything to do with it, but he said if I didn't pose for those pattycake pictures, Roger would never work in this town again.'

She thrust out her breasts and slunk across the office towards me.

'I couldn't let that happen. I'd do anything for my husband, Mr Valiant.' She stopped right in front of me and put her gloved hands on my shoulders. 'Anything.'

'What a wife,' I murmured.

You can tell me she was only a Toon but I can tell you I was only human and I couldn't resist such an invitation. I let go of my pants which I'd been holding up and they fell down around my ankles. I put my arms around her.

'I'm desperate, Mr Valiant,' she sighed, looking deep into my eyes. 'Can't you see how much I need you?'

I heard the noise of someone clearing their throat behind me. Letting go of Jessica, I swung around to find Dolores standing in the doorway glaring at us. Her timing was even better than Jessica's – or worse, depending on your point of view. Me, I wasn't sure.

'Dabblin' in watercolors, Eddie?'

I stared down at my pants, and laughed in embarrassment. Then I leaned down to pull them up – and bumped my head against Jessica's breasts. It was hard to avoid them.

'Sorry,' I mumbled.

Jessica turned on her heels and sauntered out. Passing Dolores she stopped and turned back to me.

'Goodbye, Eddie,' she breathed. 'My offer stands firm. Think about it.'

She blew me a kiss – a Toon kiss. It formed the crimson shape of her lips and floated across the room, landing on my cheek. Then she departed.

'Well!' Dolores erupted, coming over to me and yanking the kiss off my cheek. 'Do you wanna tell me what she was doin' with her arms around you?'

I didn't blame her. What could be more calculated to put Hell in a rage than woman scorned . . . in favour of a Toon?

'Probably lookin' for a good place to stick a knife!'

'Oh, come on, Eddie! I caught you with your pants down!'

There had to be some answer for that but I guess I wasn't quick enough to think of one. 'Yeah, well, if you –' I began but she'd already stormed out. 'Dolores, come –'

The bullet-ridden door minus its knob slammed behind her.

I grabbed my jacket and hat and chased after her down the stairs.

'Come on, Dolores,' I was shouting as she exited the building, 'you don't believe a painted hussy like that could turn my head.'

She was putting on her gloves and walking out into the street. I ran out after her and nearly collided with a cyclist.

'She's just trying to get her hands on the rabbit,' I said, out of breath.

Out of the corner of my eye I could see Jessica crossing her shapely legs in the back of a yellow Packard.

'That's not all she's trying to get her hands on,' Dolores shouted and marched off across the street.

'Now look, Dolores, listen,' I shouted, tagging along behind her. 'Look.' I stopped her in the middle of the road. 'I want you to go out. I want you to buy yourself a swimsuit. 'Cause you and me are goin' to Catalina. I'm on the verge of wrappin' up this case.'

'No, you're not, Eddie,' she sighed. 'That's what I came to tell you. I stopped by probate. Maroon's not after Toontown like you thought. It's Cloverleaf that wants to get their hands on Toontown. They put in the highest bid. And unless Marvin's will shows up by midnight tonight, Cloverleaf is gonna own Toontown.'

She pointed at the newly painted Cloverleaf sign above the entrance to the Terminal station.

I couldn't believe what I was hearing. 'What? At midnight tonight?'

'That's right.'

I whistled. 'First they buy the Red Car, then they want to get their hands on Toontown. I don't get it.'

Dolores was about to reply but then she stopped and put a finger to her lips. 'Shhh!'

From the nearby Terminal bar I could hear a familiar voice singing out of tune:

> *'I'm not that debonair,*
> *I'm just a silly hare!*
> *If you want class,*
> *I'll have to pass,*
> *So go get Fred Astaire!'*

That damned rabbit.

'Yeah, he's good, but . . . but can he do this?'

'Roger!' I muttered and grabbed Dolores' hand, pulling her across the street to the bar entrance.

I didn't see the cover of the manhole we'd just been standing on slide open and the heads of Smart Ass, Psycho and Greasy pop out.

Dolores did, but she didn't pay it any mind.

Why should she? After all, they were just a bunch of weasels.

10

> '*Oh, Roger is my name,*
> *And laughter is my game!*
> *Come on, cowpoke, it's just a joke!*
> *Don't sit there on your brain!*'

It was just about the worst sight I could have imagined. The patrons were crowded around the bar counter in a tight circle, clapping in time to the music and looking up at the bar. I pushed my way through the crowd and there was the rabbit dancing a jig up and down the counter.

'Whoo-hoo-hoo!' Roger shrieked as he spotted me. 'Nice shirt! Who's your tailor? Quasimodo? Whoo-hoo!'

The bar clientele seemed to think this was a great joke. I wasn't amused.

> '*My buddy's Eddie V*
> *A sourpuss, you'll see*
> *But when I'm done*
> *He'll need no gun,*
> *Cause a joker he will be, C . . .*'

He pointed at me and then turned and danced off down the other end of the bar where Angelo, the greasy moron whose mouth I'd closed with a hard-boiled egg, was sitting on a bar stool, killing himself with laughter.

The rabbit whisked Angelo's toupee off his head and twirled it around, then replaced it the wrong way round.

'... D, F, G ... H ... I!'

Angelo roared with laughter. The stupid jerk.

Meanwhile the rabbit was sliding down the length of the bar, pushing a tray in front of him.

> *'I-I-I-I-I ... love to raise some Cain!*
> *Believe me, it's no strain.*
> *It feels so great*
> *To smash a plate,*
> *And look, there ...'*

He danced along the bar, leaped up onto a tray of glasses and reached for a pile of dishes on a shelf, grabbed a dish and smashed it over his own head.

> *'... is no pain ...'*

He smashed another dish over his head as the record got stuck in the groove.

> *'... no pain ...'*

He picked up a third dish and smashed it on his head.

> *'... no pain ...'*

Fragments of china were flying around the bar.

'Ow!' Dolores screamed, as she watched her crockery being demolished, whilst her other customers were shrieking and laughing at the same time. The crazy Toon just kept smashing dishes over himself as the record kept on playing on the Victrola, with the needle stuck in the middle.

'... no pain ... no pain ... no pain ...'

I walked over to the Victrola and shoved the needle to the end of the record.

'... no –'

I yanked the dish out of his hand and pulled him over the bar by his ears. The rest of the dishes tumbled down.

'Ooooh!' Roger exclaimed as the crowd cheered, basking in the applause and grinning from floppy ear to floppy ear.

Without saying a word I marched him off to the back room and through into the secret hideaway.

'Hey, Eddie, what are y-y-y-y-y-y-ya –?'

With a grunt, I threw him across the room.

'Yi-i-i-i-ikes!' he screamed and fell head first into a bucket, sliding into the wall.

'Hey!' he shouted as I closed the secret door. 'Who turned out the lights?'

He flailed about on the floor with the bucket stuck on his head.

'I can't see a thing! What's goin' on?'

He stood up and tried to pull the bucket off his head. It refused to budge but he kept on pulling until his neck stretched to a ridiculous length.

'You crazy rabbit!' I shouted at him as he grunted and groaned. 'I've been out there risking my neck for you, and what are you doin'? Singin' and dancin'!'

He stood on his hands and tried to prise the bucket off with his feet. He finally succeeded and I just managed to catch the bucket. I threw it down and walked over to him.

'But I'm a Toon,' he protested. 'Toons are supposed to make people laugh.'

'Sit down!' I ordered.

He jumped up on a pile of soap boxes and sat down obediently.

'You don't understand,' he protested self-righteously. 'Those people needed to laugh.'

79

'Yeah, and when they're done laughing, they'll call the cops!' I reminded him angrily. 'That guy Angelo would rat on you for a nickel!'

He shook his head confidently. 'Not Angelo! He'd never turn me in.'

'Why? Because you made him laugh?'

'That's right. A laugh can be a very powerful thing.' Now he'd got up on his soap box, literally and metaphorically. 'Why, sometimes in life, it's the only weapon we have.'

A red light had started to blink in the corner. It was Dolores's way of sending me a warning.

The rabbit hadn't noticed. 'Laughter is the most imp –'

'Shhh!' I interrupted him, pointing at the red light.

I quickly removed the panel from the peephole and we crouched down and looked through into the bar.

It couldn't have been worse.

I could see him standing in the doorway, blocking out the light from the street behind him.

'I'm looking for a murderer,' said Judge Doom.

11

Behind him the Toon Squad weasels sniggered and wheezed. The bar had suddenly gone deathly quiet, the patrons going back to their tables and sitting with rapt attention.

Doom walked over to one of the tables. 'A rabbit!' he added.

He stepped up to a midget who was standing over the pile of broken dishes.

'A Toon rabbit ... about –' he shoved the midget down on to his knees '– yeah ... that big.'

'Look ... there's no rabbit here,' said Dolores from behind the bar. 'So don't harass my customers.'

Doom swung round and peered at her. 'I didn't come here to harass. I came here to reward.'

He stepped over to the blackboard on which the day's menu was chalked:

TODAY'S SPECIAL
FRENCH DIP
$.50
APPLE PIE
$.10

There was a one-armed soldier standing by the blackboard and Doom grabbed his armless sleeve and used it to wipe the chalk. It made a grating noise which made the customers wince and groan. I put my hands to my ears and the rabbit turned away, shuddering. When Doom had finished, he stepped back from his handiwork. The blackboard now read:

TODAY'S SPECIAL
RABBIT DIP
$5000

Angelo whistled and Doom turned on him.

'Hey . . . I seen a rabbit,' the scumbag blurted out.

Doom fixed him with a terrifying look.

'Where?'

Beside me Roger recoiled, gasped, gulped, then began to whimper.

'You see?' I muttered, glad at least to have proved my point.

Doom walked over to where Angelo was sitting and towered above him.

'Where?' he repeated.

'He's right here in the bar,' Angelo replied.

Doom leaned down close to him and Angelo reached back and put his arm around an imaginary rabbit.

'Well, say hello . . . Harvey.'

Everyone laughed uproariously – except Doom. Maybe he hadn't seen the movie, but he got the drift.

Roger turned and walked away smugly. 'I told you so,' he said.

Angelo was still laughing at his own genius but then Doom gave him one of his weird grins, which wiped the smile off the greasy truckdriver's face. He shut up and looked scared. Everyone else shut up too. In the silence there came a strange, scratching noise.

Doom sniffed the air curiously, then suddenly wheeled around: the record was still turning on the Victrola and the needle was scratching back and forth in the center of it. He switched it off, picked up the record and examined the label.

'"The Merry-Go-Round Broke Down",' he read and looked around at the bar patrons. 'Quite a loony selection for a group of drunken reprobates.'

The clientele, including Dolores and Angelo, were highly offended at being thus described but no one dared reply.

Doom, meanwhile, was sniffing the record and I saw a nasty grin appear on his face.

'He's here!' he announced triumphantly and sent the record soaring across the room like a discus. Stupid the weasel caught it in his mouth and Psycho, Wheezy and Smart Ass broke into raucous laughter.

'Stop that laughing!' Doom barked.

The other weasels instantly stopped, but Smart Ass kept on laughing, until Doom walked up and whacked him across the face. The weasel fell back, landing on and almost smashing the table by the peephole. He sat up with a groan and shuddered.

'Have you forgotten what happened last time?' thundered Doom, walking up to him.

I leaned my head away from the peephole as Doom drew nearer but kept listening.

'If you don't stop this laughing, you're gonna end up dead, just like your idiot hyena cousins!'

'Say, boss,' Smart Ass suggested contritely, 'you want we should disresemble the place?'

'No, Sergeant,' said Doom quietly. 'Disassembling the place won't be necessary.'

I ventured to look through the peephole again and saw him turning and walking back to the bar.

'The rabbit is going to come right to me.'

He rapped his cane on the counter to the rhythm of 'Shave-and-a-Haircut'.

I gasped. We were done for.

'No Toon can resist the old shave-and-a-haircut trick,' he said suavely.

He was peeking back through the door and rapped his cane to the same rhythm against a fire extinguisher, listening intently.

I put my hands across the peephole, trying to obliterate the deadly temptation of the rhythm as Doom kept rapping his cane.

'I don't know who's toonier,' I muttered, looking back at the rabbit, 'you or Doom.'

Roger Rabbit was standing quivering on a bar stool, his ears tied up in knots, trying to resist the lure of the rapping. At that moment I felt sorry for the sucker.

'Roger!' I hissed, trying to distract him, but he was too far gone, whimpering and grunting like crazy, like it was some deadly torment. Like I sometimes felt late at night when the last bottle was empty and the last bar was closed for business. We all have our crosses to bear.

His trembling was becoming more and more violent as the rapping of Doom's cane continued remorselessly.

'Roger, no!' I warned him.

A shadow passed over the peephole. Doom was standing directly on the other side. The rapping came through the wall, loud and clear. Roger was whimpering and quivering dementedly, his eyes turning in twirling spirals.

'Roger, no! Wait!' I hissed. 'Don't! Roger, no!'

'Shave and a haircut . . .' Doom sang through the peephole.

Roger started spinning like a top and then suddenly he flew through the air, bursting through the wall and landing in a cloud of dust at Doom's feet.

'Two bits!' he sang in a shriek, grinning and posing. The next moment Doom grabbed him by the throat, nearly strangling him as he lifted him off the floor.

The weasels had congregated around the huge hole that Roger had made in the wall and were brandishing some evil-looking knives in my direction.

I held up my hands.

'Hey, Judge, what should we do with the wallflower?' said Smart Ass.

'We'll see to him later,' Doom replied. He turned and carried Roger over to the bar. 'Right now, I feel like dispensing some justice. Bring me some Dip!'

The weasels vanished and reappeared seconds later,

carrying the barrel of bubbling liquid over to the Judge, who slipped on his black glove. He threw off the lid with one hand and held the rabbit over The Dip with the other.

Roger was screaming and shuddering, as he looked appealingly towards me, but I couldn't see how I could stop the inevitable from happening.

At the last moment, Doom seemed to relent. He pulled Roger back from the barrel and called out, 'Does the condemned have anything to say before his sentence is carried out?'

'Why, yeah –' Roger began, but then Doom tightened his grip on the rabbit's throat, strangling him and moving him over to The Dip once more.

'Whaaa!' Roger coughed and groaned.

I had joined Dolores behind the bar. I had an idea.

'Dolores,' I whispered, 'bourbon, and make it a double.'

She stared at me in horror and contempt. 'Fine time for a drink, Eddie. Maybe you'd like a bowl of pretzels to go with it!'

'Just pour the drink, Dolores,' I snapped.

She picked up a bottle of whiskey and uncorked it as Roger screeched and whined, his ears wedged against the sides of the barrel in a fruitless attempt to keep Doom from pushing him inside.

The customers, even Angelo, were looking mournful, taking off their hats out of respect for a condemned Toon.

'Hey, Judge!' I shouted out, grabbing the bottle from Dolores and pouring the whiskey into a glass.

Doom loosened his grip slightly and looked in my direction. 'Doesn't a dying rabbit deserve a last request?'

'Yeah,' Roger agreed, instantly forgetting that he was not exactly in a very good bargaining position. His nose, inches away from The Dip, was screwed up in repugnance at the foul stench.

'Nose plugs would be nice,' he suggested.

I leaned over the bar, whiskey in my hand. 'I think you want a drink,' I said to him, winking.

The stupid rabbit ignored me and carried on whimpering.

'How 'bout it, Judge, hmmm?' I said.

'Well, why not?' he grinned evilly. 'I don't mind prolonging the execution.'

He pulled Roger away from the barrel and dangled him in front of the bar.

'Uggghh!' the rabbit gasped.

I held the glass out to him. 'Happy trails.'

He gave me a resigned smile. 'No, thanks, Eddie. I'm trying to cut down.'

The klutz!

'Drink the drink!' I hissed.

'But I don't want the drink,' he insisted, pushing the glass away.

Doom smiled. 'He doesn't want the drink.'

'He does!' I shouted.

'I don't!' Roger countered.

'You do!'

'I don't!'

'You do!'

'I don't!'

'You do!'

'I don't!'

This was getting nowhere.

'You *don't*!' I said.

'I do!' denied the rabbit.

He'd fallen for it.

'You don't!' I repeated, just to make sure.

'I do!'

'You don't!'

He grabbed the drink from me.

'Listen,' he shouted. 'When I say I do, that means I do!'

I glanced back smugly at Dolores as the rabbit took a gulp, then another, and then swallowed down the whole glass.

I'd lighted the fuse. It was time to retire. I stepped back to join Dolores and watch the fireworks.

First his face changed color, going green and then purple and then black. He began to quiver violently and shriek, jerking Doom around as he prepared for take-off.

I ducked down behind the bar, grabbing Dolores and pulling her down with me as the Toon's cheeks began to inflate and his ears twirl like a propeller. Finally his head turned into a steam whistle and shot up to the roof.

'Eeeeeeeeeeeeeeeeeeeeeeeeeaaaaaaaaaaaaaaaaaaggghh!'

The customers were blown back off their stools by the force of the blast. Even Doom collapsed in a heap on the floor. As bottles and glasses exploded on the back counter, I seized my opportunity, leaping over the bar under Roger's feet, which were dangling in the air. I punched Greasy the weasel back against a table. He collapsed with a grunt. Then I turned to Stupid, and punched him in the face. He, too, groaned and fell against Doom and some of the customers who had just got back to their feet, knocking them to the floor again. I kicked Psycho across the room. He shrieked, and smashed against a table. Next came Wheezy: I bashed a chair across his face, knocking him back into a table.

'Uggh!' I felt a sharp pain in my groin. I looked down to see Smart Ass kicking me. I punched him back against the bar. Then I grabbed a beer bottle and smashed him in the face with it, just to finish him off.

Just in time, as Roger Rabbit ran out of steam and began plummeting down towards the barrel of Dip which was stationed directly beneath him, I caught him.

'Got you, kid,' I gasped, knocking over the barrel of Dip. The evil liquid began to seep across the room, and Doom and the other customers backed away from it in alarm.

'Come on, Eddie!' the rabbit shrieked, jumping out of my arms, 'let's get the hell outta here!'

He ran across the room to the exit, bumping into two startled old men who were just coming up the stairs. I chased after him as Roger shoved the old men out of the way.

'Move it, pops!' he shouted, running down the stairs and into the street. 'Yi-i-ikes!'

I caught up with him outside where he was busily bumping into pedestrians.

'That was quick thinking, Eddie,' he said happily. 'Nothin' like usin' the old spine flower, the wise noodle, the smart puddin' –!'

'Roger!' I shouted, grabbing him by the ears and yanking him back to the Toon Squad paddy wagon, which was parked at the curb.

'Yi-i-ikes!'

'Let's use this!' I muttered, opening the driver's door and throwing him into the back. 'Let's get outta here! What are ya waitin' for?'

I climbed into the driver's seat and reached for the ignition. Then I cursed. 'There's no damn key!'

'Hey, you weasels,' came a voice from the back of the paddy wagon, 'let me outta here, willya? Come on, I gotta make a livin'!'

'Benny, is that you?' said the Rabbit, opening a panel behind him and peering into the back.

'No,' said Benny, 'it's Eleanor Roosevelt. Come on, Roger, get me outta here!'

As the rabbit squeezed through the panel opening, his 'love letter' to Jessica slipped out of his pants. I caught it as Roger popped his head through the panel.

'Eddie, we got ourselves a ride!' he shouted excitedly. 'Open the doors!'

What did I have to lose? I tucked the letter in my pocket and climbed out of the paddy wagon.

12

'Benny', if you haven't guessed, turned out to be a Toon taxi-cab, a yellow affair with a voice like a cab's hooter and a personality to match. Just try taking a cab down Broadway in the rush hour, crank up the pressure a few million times and that was Benny. I'd thought the rabbit was hyper but the cab was a Toon beyond even Marvin's wildest imaginings. The simplest way to describe him was manic-depressive but without the depressive bit.

'Pheww!' sighed the rabbit, sitting in the driver's seat as Benny backed out of the paddy wagon and drew up alongside me.

'Phew! Ah, that's better!' honked Benny. 'Can't believe they locked me up for drivin' on the sidewalk.'

'Come on, Eddie, get in!'

'It was just a couple of miles,' Benny went on.

'I'll drive,' I insisted, shoving Roger aside and getting into Benny's driver's seat.

'But I wanna drive,' said the rabbit.

'I'll drive,' Benny announced. 'I'm the cab.'

He immediately made a U-turn in the street, nearly running over a pedestrian.

'Outta my way, pencil neck!' he honked. 'How about this weather, huh?' he inquired in cabbie fashion as he zigzagged down the street. 'It never rains!'

Behind us I could see the weasels emerging from the Terminal Bar, pointing at us and climbing into the paddy wagon.

'And how about those Brooklyn Dodgers?' Benny hooted as he passed a car on the right. 'Are they bums or what?'

'Benny, Eddie, we got company!' said the rabbit, pointing at the paddy wagon which had swerved into the street in pursuit.

Benny was busy doing what he did worst. 'Will you look at those two –' he grumbled as two cars ahead of him drove at a perfectly respectable speed along their lanes. He swerved, accelerated and drove straight down the broken line between them.

'Excuse me, ladies, I have to make a living here.'

Roger screamed and I began to feel queasy.

'Now that's what I call a couple of road hogs.'

The paddy wagon was making steady progress behind us and suddenly I heard gunshots. As Roger cowered in fear, I looked back to see Smart Ass pointing a gun out the window at us.

More shots were fired but they missed us and the rabbit, who had closed his eyes and placed his hands over his ears, opened them and shrieked.

'Benny, look out for the Red –'

Benny was hurtling us down a steep hill and at the intersection I could see a streetcar crossing directly ahead of us.

'– Ca-a-a-a-a-r!' screamed the rabbit, his eyes bugging out of his head.

I was screaming myself as Benny, far from reducing his speed, accelerated towards the streetcar. At the last moment, mere inches away from the Red Car, Benny screeched to a stop and spun round, skidding to the left before driving off again. The rabbit was nearly thrown out of Benny: he seemed to dangle in the air before hurtling back into the cab. While the Toon Squad had been left behind for the time being, trouble was coming from a new quarter.

Behind us I could see a couple of motorcycle cops emerging from around a corner and speeding after us.

The rabbit was now hanging from the back of Benny, swinging around wildly on his extended arms. 'Benny!' he shrieked. 'There's cops right behind us!'

Without hesitating, Benny backed up into an alley, flinging Roger off into the road. He ran after the cab and jumped back inside.

'Not for long, Roger!' Benny hooted, as the cops turned into the alley. He began to speed in reverse down the alley. 'Now they're right in front of us!'

'Benny-y-y-y-y!' I screamed.

'Eddie,' yelled the rabbit, 'we're goin' backwards. Turn us around!'

As though the decision was up to me!

'Give me the wheel!' he shouted, grabbing the steering wheel from me.

'Roger!' I shouted back, trying to wrest it back from him, but he had already turned it sharply and Benny suddenly swerved and spun around a few times before heading down the alley again, this time in forward gear.

'The cops are still on our tail!' Roger yelled.

'I know the cops are on our tail,' I snapped. 'What do you think I am, bli –'

At that moment the paddy wagon appeared at the other end of the alley, which meant that we were now sandwiched between the Toon Squad and the motorbike cops.

'Yeo-o-o . . .' Roger screamed.

'Oh, no!' I moaned as the rabbit grabbed me around the neck.

I could see the weasels laughing and brandishing their revolvers as we roared towards them.

'Pull the lever!' Benny ordered.

The rabbit and I stared at each other, baffled.

'Which one?' we screamed in unison.

We stared at the array of buttons and dials on Benny's dashboard.

'Which one?' Benny repeated, and then a sign popped up out of a panel:

THIS LEVER, STUPID ———→

The sign pointed towards the only lever on the dashboard. We were now less than twenty feet from the paddy wagon and heading straight towards it. I pulled the lever and Benny began to rise into the air on a set of extension legs until we were high above the Toon Squad and the cops, who were all staring up at us in amazement and fury.

We emerged from the alley into the street, stopping an oncoming car as we sailed around the corner.

'I'm gettin' too old for this!' Benny hooted, raising one set of his wheels as he moved over a parked car, then lowering them as we sped down the street.

Behind us we heard a crash as the paddy wagon collided with the motorbike cops, but we now had a new problem to contend with. The suspension legs had not retracted and we were still flying above the street – and heading for . . .

'Jumpin' jeep –' Roger gasped.

'Hey, Roger?' Benny honked. 'What do you call the middle of a song?'

'Gee, I don't know,' the rabbit mused, then he shrieked, leaping on to my shoulders and shouted, 'A bri-i-i-i-dge!'

We were flying at the level of a bridge overpass and I could make out a woman standing on it with a baby carriage. She ducked in terror as Benny headed towards the bridge and I was just thinking how I should have made a will and maybe donated a few dollars towards the upkeep of Doom's Dip when Benny flew onto the bridge, retracted his legs and made a landing of sorts, breaking through a road barrier, speeding into the opposite lane and tearing across the bridge as oncoming cars were forced to a stop, honking their horns at us.

Benny laughed. 'Well, fellas, where can I drop ya?'

'Somewhere we can hide,' said Roger, climbing off my shoulders and ducking below the dashboard.

'I got just the place,' said Benny, changing over to the

outside lane. 'And incidentally, if you should ever need a ride, just stick out your thumb. Hey, share the road, willya, lady?'

He swerved in front of another car in the adjacent lane, forcing it to brake to a halt.

Somehow, that was one offer I didn't think I'd be taking up for a while.

13

The door opened and there was Goofy, who instantly fell flat on his face.

'Now that wasn't so bad, was it?' came the cheery voice of the narrator and the audience broke into laughter.

Goofy was now struggling with an exercise spring which catapulted him into the air. He grabbed some gymnastic rings and swung back and forth, each time crashing into the ceiling.

While Roger Rabbit sat killing himself with laughter and munching popcorn in the front of the movie theater balcony, I sat in the back, fuming. We were the only two in the balcony, but the rabbit's enthusiasm made up for it.

'Boy, did you see that?' he giggled, turning back to me. 'Nobody takes a wallop like Goofy.'

Goofy was being catapulted through the skylight, into another house and out an upstairs window.

'What timing! What finesse! What a genius! Oouch!'

I'd had enough of Goofy and the rabbit. I walked down to his seat, yanked him by the ears and replaced him in a seat next to mine.

'We're supposed to be hiding!' I growled. 'What's wrong with you?'

'What's wrong with *you*?' the rabbit retorted. 'You're the only person in this theatre that isn't laughing. Is there nothing that can permeate your impervious puss?'

I wiped Roger's spit from my face as the ridiculous Toon began pulling funny faces.

'Hey, Eddie!'

He made some kind of a noise that was supposed to make me laugh.

'Boy, nothin',' he sighed. 'What could have possibly happened to you to turn you into such a sourpuss?'

I held my breath. 'You wanna know?' I said grimly. 'I'll tell you. A Toon killed by brother.'

The rabbit's face fell. 'A Toon? No.'

'That's right. A Toon.' I sighed. 'We were investigating a robbery at the First National Bank of Toontown. Back in those days, me and Teddy liked workin' Toontown.' I gave a wry chuckle. 'We thought it was a lot of laughs. Anyway . . .'

I took a bottle of whiskey out of my pocket, yanked the cork off and took a swig. '. . . this guy . . . got away with a zillion simoleons. We trailed him to a little dive down on Yockster Street. We went in. Only he got the drop on us. Literally.' I sighed again. It was still something I didn't like to think about too much – or too hard.

'Dropped a piano on us from fifteen storeys. Broke my arm. Teddy never made it. I never did find out who that guy was. All I remember was . . . he was standin' over me, laughin' . . . with those burnin' red eyes . . . and that high, squeaky voice. He disappeared into Toontown after that.'

I looked across at the rabbit. He was sobbing loudly and had grabbed hold of his own ears like they were two handkerchiefs.

'No wonder you hate me,' he sobbed. 'If a Toon killed my brother . . . I'd hate me, too.'

I returned the whiskey bottle to my pocket and patted him. 'Come on, don't cry. I don't hate you.'

'Yes, you do,' he insisted, still sobbing.

'No, I don't.'

'You do hate me. Otherwise you wouldn't have yanked my ears all those times.'

I hadn't counted on the rabbit being so sensitive. Maybe I had been too hard on him. After all, he'd been through a lot recently, what with Jessica playing pattycake and Doom playing Dip. He'd been looking to me for a bit of kindness and I'd let him down.

'Well,' I muttered. 'I'm – I'm . . . sorry I yanked your ears.'

He stopped sobbing all at once, and looked at me with hope shining in his dopey eyes.

'All the times you yanked my ears?'

'All the times I yanked your ears.'

He held out his hand to me to shake. 'Apology accepted. Put 'er there, pal. I feel better . . .'

He turned back to the screen and grinned as a new film started to play. Then still gripping my hand and as I struggled to free myself, he suddenly leaped over the rows of seats towards the balcony rail.

'Oh, boy! I hope it's another cartoon,' he exclaimed, full of anticipation.

'Jeepers!' he shouted out. Another stupid newsreel. I hate the news!'

I saw someone walking down the aisle from the balcony doorway and turned.

'Did you get all the stuff?' I asked as Dolores seated herself next to me.

'Yes,' she said. 'It's all packed up in the car.'

'. . . in Atlantic City,' the news commentator was reading, 'the Shriners' March. Wearing their fezzes and bright uniforms, they parade before a hundred thousand spectators as a highlight of the Shrine Convention.'

'I woulda been here right after you called,' she said, 'but I had to shake the weasels.'

'Yeah,' I said. 'I'm sorry about the trouble in the bar.'

'. . . That's the gay side,' went on the announcer. 'There's a serious side when Imperial Potentate George H. Row of Buffalo urged all Shriners to help halt the spread of Communism.'

'Oh, hell,' Dolores laughed. 'Stuffin' olives wasn't for me anyway.'

I looked at her. She was still young, and still one hell of a good-looker. What was she doing with a bum like me?

'Dolores? You oughta find yourself a good man.'

She smiled and pressed my arm. 'But I already have a good man.'

'... Many cities are represented in the march, and many temples, as the Imperial Council meets once again.'

There was a new item on the newsreel: a young girl with an apple on her head was having knives thrown at her.

Dolores leaned closer to kiss me.

'... It takes a steady eye and a stout heart to heave knives at the apple of your eye but this female William Tell has no qualms...'

In the front row, Roger had turned and was gazing at us. His ears were twisted into the shape of a heart and there were valentines in his eyes.

'P-p-p-lease, don't mind me,' he grinned.

Dolores and I exchanged exasperated looks.

'... and plenty of faith,' carried on the announcer.

'You'd better get going, Eddie,' Dolores said.

Roger was up like a shot. He leapt up the aisle, unhooked the balcony rope and sped through the exit.

'... a near miss,' went on the announcer. 'But this miss says that's as good as a smile...'

Dolores and I started walking up the aisle and Roger rejoined us. The newsreel had cut from the 'William Tell' girl to footage of Maroon Cartoon Studios, but I wasn't really paying much attention. We were getting out of all this and in a few days' time it would just seem like a bad dream. Still, I wondered what my brother would have thought of me.

'I'm glad Teddy's not here to see me runnin' away with my tail between my legs,' I muttered.

'It's not so bad once you get used to it,' said the rabbit philosophically.

'... Dateline: Hollywood, California,' the announcer went on. 'Cloverleaf Oil was on the move this week, acquiring two Hollywood institutions –'

I snorted with disgust. What Cloverleaf got up to had ceased to be of any interest to me.

'– The Pacific Red Car Trolley Line, and the venerated Maroon Cartoon Studios. Here, R.K. Maroon is seen clinching the deal with Cloverleaf's bankers and execs in one of the biggest real-estate deals ever in California history.'

It was the last sentence that stuck in my mind. Why hadn't I seen what was as plain as the shining red nose on Roger Rabbit's face? I was just about to go through the exit doors: I re-entered the cinema and was in time to see the shots of Maroon shaking hands with some banker types who were giving him a check.

'... Three and a half million dollars for a laugh factory – and that's no joke...'

'That's it!' I gasped. 'That's the connection!'

14

'Let's forget it!' said Roger Rabbit, as I drew Dolores's car up in front of the gates of the Maroon Cartoon Studio and turned into the lot. But I wasn't backing out now even if the rabbit was chicken: he was hiding on the floor and quivering like jelly.

'There's nobody here,' he objected.

I gazed up at the deserted building, illuminated in the night-time sky, remembering the chaos of humans and Toons on my previous visit. But I hadn't come back for a rendezvous with a bunch of musical chairs or cows or an ostrich or Dumbo: my business was with one man and I had a pretty good idea he'd show up.

'Is that it,' I said, 'or are you scared?'

The rabbit sat up. 'P-p-p-please, me scared?' He opened the car door. 'Don't be ridiculous.'

His teeth were chattering like a chorus line's tapshoes in some Astaire musical.

'When you called Maroon,' said the rabbit as we climbed out of the car, 'you told him you had the will, but you don't. When he finds out, he's gonna be mad. He might try to kill you.'

I moved towards the outer wall of the building, with the rabbit close behind me. If I'd had a tail, he would have been stepping on it.

'I can handle a Hollywood cream puff,' I muttered. 'I just don't want the odds to change, so you cover my back.'

I moved towards the stairs and walked up a few steps. Then I turned back to Roger. 'And if you hear or see anything,' I whispered, 'beep the horn twice.'

I climbed the stairs, leaving Roger outside in the lot...

'Yeah, that's it,' Roger Rabbit mumbled, talking aloud to keep his spirits up. 'Beep the horn twice. Cover your back.'

He stuck up two fingers of each hand as if they were guns. 'OK, I'm ready. Dukes up... eyes peeled... ears to the ground. Why, nobody gets the drop on Roger Rabbit –'

Behind him a frying pan smashed down on his head. He groaned, stiffened and fell straight back. Then he was dragged around the corner...

I came in through the door to the cutting-room rather than the main door to Maroon's office. I'd noticed it on my previous visit and decided it might be just as well to come in the back way, just in case he was planning any little surprises for me, like dropping a sofa on my head.

He was standing checking his watch, still looking like a bloodhound in need of exercise. Perhaps something could be arranged.

I tapped him on the back. He jumped. The guy was nervous.

'What's up, Doc?'

'Valiant, what are you tryin' to do, give me a heart attack?'

'You need a heart before you can have a heart attack.'

'Yeah, yeah, yeah. You got the will?'

There was no doubt about it. He was on edge, like he wanted to take a walk real bad.

'Sure.' I reached into my trenchcoat breast pocket and showed him the corner of a document. 'I got the will.' I closed my trenchcoat protectively and eyed the liquor tray. 'The question is, do you have the way?' I strolled towards the decanters. ''Cause I can tell you now, it ain't gonna come cheap.'

Maroon stared at me. I think he was actually impressed. 'You got a lot of brass, coming up here by yourself!'

'Who said I'm here by myself?'

Down in the studio lot Jessica Rabbit paused to catch her breath. It had been heavy work loading Roger into the trunk of her Packard, but at least he was out cold.

She slammed the door of the trunk shut, stuffed the frying pan into her tiny bag and strolled off to the front of her car.

It was a pity it had to be this way, but she couldn't afford to take any chances . . .

'OK, hardcase,' Maroon said in a low voice. 'How much?'

I paused, playing for time.

'Give a girl a chance to think,' I said, pouring myself a Scotch. 'Let's see. Your take is three and a half million dollars.'

I gazed out at the lot from the window. There was no sign of the rabbit. He must have been waiting at the stairway entrance.

'Let me see the will,' said Maroon behind me.

'I told you, I got it.'

'I wanna see it . . . now.'

Maroon really was a very impatient fellow. He spun me around, knocking the drink out of my hand, and I still hadn't even had a sip. He grabbed the 'will' out of my pocket, unfolded it and studied it.

Which gave me just enough time to reach back for a seltzer bottle.

'"How I do love thee?"' he began reading and faltered. 'This supposed to be a joke?'

He crumpled up the letter and stuffed it in my trouser pocket.

'No,' I replied. 'But this is.'

I held up the seltzer bottle and squirted him in the face. When he stood there gargling, I punched him twice, once on

101

the cheek, once on the jaw. He must have been taking lessons from Goofy or the rabbit, because he collapsed like a Toon. All that was missing were the stars around his head.

'Get up!' I snapped, pointing my pistol at him. 'Come on.'

'Well,' he groaned. 'What are you gonna do to me, Valiant?'

He climbed painfully to his feet and I grabbed him by his maroon necktie.

'I'm gonna listen to you spin the Cloverleaf scenario,' I said. 'The story of greed, sex and murder.'

I pulled him over to the moviola. 'And the parts that I don't like,' I added, 'I'm gonna edit out.'

'You've got it all wrong,' he whimpered. 'I'm a cartoon maker, not a murderer.'

'Everybody's gotta have a hobby!' I said, and pulled on his tie, tightening it around his neck.

He choked a bit, which I figured would give him a foretaste, a kind of trailer for the main feature. He was forced to lean his head forward and I inserted the necktie into the moviola and stepped on the foot pedal.

'Aagh! Stop it! Stop it! Stop it!' he gagged as the tie started to take a ride on the moviola.

I eased up on the pedal.

'The truth is,' he gasped, 'I had a chance to sell my studio, but Cloverleaf wouldn't buy my property unless Marvin sold them his. The stubborn bastard wouldn't sell! So I was gonna blackmail Marvin with pictures of him and the rabbit's wife. Blackmail, that's all! I've been around Toons all my life! I didn't want to see 'em destroyed!'

What was he saying? This was a new angle to the story.

'Toons destroyed?' I said. 'Why?'

'If I tell you, I'm a dead man,' he groaned.

I kicked down the moviola. 'You're a dead man if you don't tell me.'

Suddenly something caught my eye: it was a framed cartoon poster opposite the window, of a mouse holding a revolver – except that right over the drawing of the revolver I could see a real revolver, or rather the *reflection* of a real revolver, which was being pointed into the office from behind the curtain at the window. I glanced at the window and saw the barrel of a gun pointing at me – or maybe it was pointing at Maroon, it was hard to be sure.

'... Unless Marvin's will shows,' Maroon was saying, 'by midnight tonight, Toontown's gonna be land for the free –'

Just in time, I ducked out of the way as gunshot – a series of shots – blasted repeatedly into Maroon's back; then, as the barrel of the gun turned to point at me, I rolled across the floor and crouched behind a chair.

Bullets tore through the upholstery, perforating the walls. What the rabbit had left undamaged during his drinking spree, the gunman finished off. Maroon and his office were blitzed.

With a final salvo of gunfire, the gun barrel retreated through the Venetian blinds. An uncanny silence descended on the office.

After a minute I ventured out from behind the chair. I pointed my gun at the window, but whoever had been there had vanished. Then I checked out Maroon.

He lay across the moviola, his tie still caught up in the mechanism. If he'd been a Toon, he'd have got up and danced.

But he wasn't and he didn't.

He was very, very dead.

15

I took one more look through the blinds.

I didn't like what I saw.

I had liked it when I'd seen it in the Ink and Paint Club when it sang and danced – but that was two dead bodies ago.

Jessica Rabbit was running across the lot. She disappeared down an alley.

As I ran down the stairs I found my mind filling up with questions and running out of answers.

What had Maroon meant by his last words: *by midnight tonight Toontown's gonna be land for the free?* Whose gun had shot him? If it wasn't Jessica Rabbit, what was she doing on the Maroon lot? And what had become of Roger Rabbit?

At the bottom of the stairs I was in time to see Jessica's yellow Packard speeding across the lot. I ran to Dolores's car, already knowing that the rabbit would not be there, but I called out his name in the vain hope he'd be hiding under the seat.

He wasn't.

I climbed in and tore off in pursuit of Jessica. I could see the Packard in the distance, but then lost sight of her as a Red Car crossed an intersection. I spotted her again as the Packard sped around a hairpin turn and held her in my sights as I followed her around the curve.

Then I saw a painted sign which sent a shiver down my spine:

TOONTOWN

$\longleftarrow$ ——————

In the distance, beckoning like the jaws of Hell, I could see the Toontown Tunnel, and when Jessica's Packard disappeared into it, I knew I was in deep, deep trouble.

A hundred yards before the tunnel I brought the car to a screeching halt. I climbed out, walked round to the front of the car and gazed at the entrance to the tunnel. I realised that the moment of truth had arrived. At the back of my mind, beneath all the immediate questions, was a bigger question which I had been shelving ever since that night when a Toon killed my brother.

One way or another I knew that the answer lay at the other end of that tunnel. I felt angry. Angrier than I had ever felt in my life. If I hadn't felt so angry, my fear would have got the better of me and I'd have driven away from Toontown for ever. But as it was, I really had no choice.

I took off my trenchcoat and threw it in the car. Then I walked back again to the front of the car, and stared once more at the tunnel, with the gun in my hand.

I couldn't turn back now.

I tossed my gun onto the front seat of the car, then from out of the back, I pulled my briefcase and opened it up. Inside was my guncase. I lifted the lid, glancing at the plaque on the inside:

> Thanks for getting me
> out of the Hoosegow.
> Yosemite Sam

I took out the Toon revolver, held it up and examined it. It felt good and I even found myself smiling. Then I opened up a

105

small compartment at the bottom of the guncase. I hadn't seen those six Toon bullets for maybe five years or more.

The bullets were dressed like Western gunslingers and one Red Indian. They were snoring loudly, as I opened the case; then, one by one, they woke up, all talking at once:

'What...?'

'Yeah, what in the Sam Hill...?'

'Ooh, what the...? Eddie Valiant? Well, you're a sight for sore eyes.'

'I ain't seen you nigh onto five years.'

'Where you been?'

'Drunk,' I replied to the final question. 'You feelin' frisky tonight, fellas?'

'Yeah!' they shouted, laughing and cheering.

Satisfied, I lowered the revolver and opened the cylinder.

'Let's go,' I commanded.

One by one the bullets leaped into their respective chambers, laughing and hollering. I closed the cylinder. Then I took out a pint bottle of whiskey, bit off the cork and raised the bottle to my lips.

Suddenly the sheer stupidity of this act stopped me in mid-track. I stared at the bottle, hesitated for a moment and then poured the whiskey out on the road. Then I hurled the bottle as far and as high as it would go, aimed my Toon revolver at it and fired.

The Indian bullet shot out of the revolver: it stopped in mid-air for a moment then flew off towards the bottle, which had reached its zenith.

'Ya-ya-ya-ya-ya-ya-ya-ya-ya-ya-ya-ya!' it hollered, then pulled out an enormous tomahawk and smashed the bottle, while letting out an Indian war-cry: 'Woo-woo-woo-woo-woo-woo-woo-woo!'

I climbed back into the car, put it in gear and started into the Toontown Tunnel. I shone the headlights on the walls, getting ready for the extraordinary metamorphosis which I knew was coming.

If you haven't been to Toontown, maybe I can describe it like this. Imagine you're in bed. It's a pitch dark night and though your eyes are open you can't see a thing. You lie there and you're not sure whether you're awake or asleep. Then suddenly you think, I must be asleep 'cause otherwise why am I dreaming in Technicolor and not just Technocolor but cartoon color? You're inside a cartoon landscape where there are no greys, no shades, no soft edges. You're inside an animated movie and that's Toontown. And there's one other thing: in Hollywood, the Toons have to do what the humans tell them, but in Toontown the Toons make up the laws of nature as they go along.

So there I was driving towards the red curtain which was the tunnel exit. As I approached the curtain it rose up to reveal the Toontown countryside. Suddenly I was inside it and driving down a cartoon dirt road past patchwork-quilt hills, singing trees and picturebook mushrooms. A huge orange sun popped up over the horizon, like the kind of sun you always imagined when you were a kid, like some big balloon. The sun was bouncing up and down and singing along with the trees, because everything and everyone sings in Toontown.

> '*Smile, darn ya, smile!*
> *You know this old world*
> *Is a great world, after all . . .*

And all the while the Crazy Trees sang along in a kind of bass line:

> '*Bl-bl-bl-bl-bluh!*'

Suddenly the Toontown countryside was full of Toons: some I knew from the movies; others I thought I might have seen but couldn't be sure; still others were complete strangers, who'd maybe lived all their life in Toontown without making a movie. There were hordes of baby Mickey Mouses, gophers, rabbits and flying cupids and they all sang along:

> '*Smile, darn ya, smile!*
> *And right away*

> *Watch Lady Luck*
> *Pay you a call.'*

More and more Toons kept appearing, like the Three Little
Pigs, the Reluctant Dragon, a group of dancing goblins,
Jimmy Cricket, and they all joined in.

> *'Things are never black as they are painted.*
> *Time for you and joy to get acquainted.'*

Three hummingbirds were flying around the car windshield, making it difficult for me to see where I was going.

'Hi, Eddie,' they sang in unison, while the chorus of Toons
and Trees kept on singing, 'Make life worthwhile . . .'

Suddenly the hummingbirds flew off to the back of the car
and hovered outside the rear windshield. I turned around to
look at them.

'Bye, Eddie,' they sang, and flew away.

The next moment, the car crashed into something, throwing
me against the steering wheel. Steam shot out of the hood.

I was in a limbo, unable to see in front of me and too shocked
to turn round.

16

At last I poked my head out of the side window. One thing was for sure – I'd left the countryside behind and was now in some kind of cartoon city landscape. Then I saw Jessica's Packard, smashed up against a large dump truck labelled, 'OVER-USED GAGS'. A tiny wind-up toy was toddling around next to the wreck, and a bowling ball rolled out of the dump truck and crushed it.

I climbed out of the car and saw immediately that it had smashed into the rear of Jessica's Packard. I was about to inspect the damage when a cartoon fire engine suddenly appeared out of nowhere, swerving past me at a crazy speed, sounding its siren and bell. Mr Toad was riding on top of its high extension ladder, and shouting, 'Tally ho! Tally ho!'

All around me Toons were chasing each other through squalid urban cartoon streets and buildings, fighting with and shouting at each other.

I looked inside the Packard and as I leaned back out of the car a circle of tweeting birds flew around my head.

'Get outta here!' I shouted, chasing them away and swatting one across the head.

Then I noticed a familiar silhouette in the upper-floor

window of a tall, nearby building. I figured that it was time to get a few answers and Jessica Rabbit might just be the one to supply them.

I walked into the lobby and pressed the elevator button and then recoiled as I realised it was the nose on a Toon face. I looked up at the floor indicator and watched as the dial moved in a matter of seconds from '450' to '1' as the elevator dived from the top to the bottom of the building. As it landed on the ground floor, the crash sent shock waves all around me. The earth seemed to move beneath my feet and the Toon elevator itself looked badly shaken.

The doors swung open and Droopy the dog stood there, doubling as an elevator attendant.

'Going up, sir?' he said wearily.

I nodded and stepped inside . . . and into thin air.

There was no ground beneath my feet and I dropped several feet below the lobby floor. I gasped, looking up at Droopy who, I now saw, was standing on a very tall crate.

'Mind the step, sir,' he said. His timing left a lot to be desired.

I got to my feet and glared at him as he started to close the elevator doors.

'Hold on, sir,' he said, pulling down hard on the control lever.

The force of the lift-off sent me reeling back on the floor as the elevator shot up the building.

I dimly caught sight of the Road Runner and Coyote shooting by somewhere between the 20th and 30th floors but since I'd been flattened into a pancake by the blast-off I didn't pay much attention.

Without any warning Droopy suddenly stopped the elevator, sending me flying up to the ceiling.

'Your floor, sir,' he announced indifferently. 'Have a good day, sir,' he added as I dropped out of the elevator, landing on the hallway floor.

A moment later he and the elevator shot back down again.

Bruised and shaken, I walked along the hallway, peering through keyholes. At last, I found what I was looking for.

Though she had her back to me I recognised that magnificent physique at once. She was standing at the far end of the apartment, and from my keyhole vantage point she appeared to be selecting lingerie.

'Gotcha,' I muttered.

I stood up and to my surprise the door creaked open. It was then that she turned round. To my horror, I saw that it was not Jessica Rabbit at all.

She was hideously ugly with the face of a demented hyena.

A ma-a-a-a-n!' she screamed, smacking her lips and running towards me, her arms outstretched.

I quickly slammed the door on her and turned to flee as her lips burst through the door, and the sound of her smacking lips resonated through the building. She smashed through the door, stretching her arms out to me and screamed in a piercing voice, 'Yoo-hoo, lover boy! It's me!'

I tore into the men's room, slamming the door shut behind me. A sign dangled from the doorknob:

OUT OF ORDER

As I turned away from the door to catch my breath, I noticed the shattered remains of a bathroom wall next to the door. Graffiti was scribbled next to the towel dispenser:

FOR A GOOD TIME
CALL
ALLYSON 'WONDERLAND'
THE BEST IS YET
TO BE

I looked down and screamed in terror: what I had thought was the door to the men's room was simply a door. I was standing on a narrow ledge and beneath me a sheer drop of thousands of feet. Far below me I could see a plane flying through a thick bank of clouds beneath which Toontown itself was barely visible. Then I lost my balance and plummeted down.

'Uuuuuuuuuuuuuggggggghhhhhh!'

At least I had enough wits to grab my hat. I need my hat. It helps me to think. Not that it's possible to make many useful plans when you're falling off a skyscraper, but you might just remember to say your prayers which can be helpful if you're counting on getting into heaven. Me, I passed on that one and thought of Dolores.

And then, to my complete and utter fury, Roger Rabbit came klutzing and clowning into my mind. I just couldn't seem to get away from the rabbit. Even now.

If you don't have a good sense of humor, you're better off dead.

A laugh can be a very powerful thing. Why, sometimes in life, it's the only weapon we have.

OK, rabbit, I thought, have it your way.

I laughed ... And I laughed ... And then I shrieked ...

My fall had been interrupted by a flagpole that stuck out from the side of the building.

I bounced up and down with it as it wiggled. Being a Toon flagpole it made a big deal of this bouncing business, giving me a thorough workout. And just when I was trying to work out my next move, a little bird popped out of a nest on the flagpole and walked along it until it came to my hand which was, of course, by this time getting very tired of hanging on.

So the bird steps on my hand.

'Oh, look, piggies!' she tweeted.

'Hi, Tweety,' I greeted her dourly.

She pulled up my index finger.

'This little piggy went to market.'

'No,' I cajoled.

'This little piggy stayed home,' she tweeted, pulling up my middle finger.

'Not now, Tweety.'

She moved on to my ring finger.

'This little piggy had roast beef. And ...'

I had one finger left.

'DON'T YOU TOUCH THAT FINGER, YOU –'

'... this little piggy had –'

I dropped like a stone from the flagpole as Tweety sighed,

'Uh-oh, ran out of piggies.'

Suddenly I was not alone in my free fall.

Mickey Mouse and Bugs Bunny floated up towards me and joined me on either side. Both were carrying unopened parachutes on their backs. Mickey was whistling, while Bugs was chomping on a carrot.

'Ehh, what's up, Doc?' he greeted me cheerfully. 'Jumpin' without a parachute? Kinda dangerous, ain't it?'

'Yeah,' I agreed.

'Yeah,' chuckled Mickey. 'You could get killed.'

'You guys got a spare?'

'Uh, Bugs does,' said Mickey.

'Yeah?'

'Yeah,' said Bugs, 'but I don't think you want it.'

'I do!' I shouted, 'I do! Give it to me!'

Mickey Mouse chortled. 'Gee, uh, better let him have it, Bugs.'

Bugs Bunny shrugged. 'OK, Doc. Whatever you say. Here's the spare.'

He pulled out his other parachute pack and handed it to me, then they both released their parachutes and floated up and away from me before I could say thanks.

I released the parachute – and to my dismay discovered that there was only a rubber tire inside.

'Aw, poor fella,' chuckled Mickey Mouse above me.

'Yeah,' said Bugs Bunny. 'Ain't I a stinker?'

'Oh, no!' I screamed, letting go of the tire as I kept on plummeting.

I could now see most of Toontown spread before me, and every second it grew bigger, like a mouth that was opening up to swallow me. Then I saw there really was a mouth opening up to swallow me and attached to it were pair of lips that were smacking hungrily and a pair of outstretched arms and –

The ugly broad caught me in her arms. It was a fate worse than death.

'My man!' she howled and before I could get away, she gave me a big wet kiss on the cheek. It felt like my face was being put through a food mixer.

'Uuuuugghh!' I screamed and then she pulled her lips off my cheek which sent me tumbling head over heels down the street.

I lay in the gutter and raised my head. At the far end of the street I saw her, arms outstretched, rushing towards me.

'Come to Mama!' she howled.

With no time to consider whether I might be violating the Toontown traffic regulations, I pulled up the divider line from the street, tearing it off the ground like a long band of sticky tape, and ripped it into two. As she howled and laughed her way towards me I carried the loose end of the divider line to the sidewalk and tossed it against a brick wall. Like a bull to a red flag, that broad came roaring up the dividing line and followed it headlong into the wall.

'Toons,' I muttered, gazing at the hole in the bricks. 'Gets 'em every time.'

At the end of the wall was a dark, dingy alley. Night had fallen – the laws of day and night in Toontown, if you haven't guessed, are quite elastic and depend on what cartoon you happen to be in – and there was no one in sight. I reached for the Toon revolver in my jacket and walked on down the alley, past a 'Porky's All Beef Sausage' handbill.

I wrinkled up my nose and sneezed.

'Gesundheit,' said my elongated shadow along the wall.

'Thanks,' I said.

She was standing at the end of the alley. The real Jessica Rabbit – as real as she could ever be, that is. Her gun was pointed at me, which didn't surprise me too much.

'Valiant,' she called out.

I raised my hands, unaware of the long pointed shadow that had suddenly appeared on the wall behind me.

'I always knew I'd get it in Toontown,' I shouted.

'Behind you!' Jessica shouted the warning – and fired.

I spun round and it was then that I saw a shadow that wasn't mine. A second later the shadow disappeared as Jessica's bullet met its mark.

Or had it? Maybe I was the mark. Maybe she was a bad shot.

'Drop it, lady!' I snapped.

114

She raised her hands and slunk up the alley towards me.

'I just saved your life and you still don't trust me?' she called out.

'I don't trust anybody or anything.'

'Not even your own eyes?'

I looked down: at my feet lay a gun that somehow looked familiar.

'That's the gun that killed R.K. Maroon, and Doom pulled the trigger,' she said, walking up to me.

'Doom?'

'I followed him to the studio, but I was too late to stop him.'

'That's right!' came Doom's rasping voice from behind me.

I swung round and saw him. He was now the Running Corpse, heading up the alley towards us.

'You'll never stop me!' he jeered. 'You're dead! You're both dea-a-ad!'

'Doom!' I shouted and pointing my Toongun at him, I fired three times.

He ran around a corner and my bullets gave chase, screeching to a stop where the Judge had taken a right turn.

'Which way did he go?' asked one of the bullets.

'Well, I don't know,' replied a second. Then the stupid Toon-bullet pointed to the left, 'Well, he went that-a-way.'

'Then let's go!' screamed the first, and all three bullets tore off in the wrong direction.

I shook my head at Jessica. 'Dum dums,' I sighed, throwing the Toongun away.

'Come on,' she said, taking my arm.

'Yeah,' I replied.

We reached the end of the alley and stopped. Jessica stared in dismay at her wrecked Packard. I noticed that the trunk was now open. It had been closed when I'd smashed into it.

'Oh, no,' she sighed. 'Where's Roger?'

'Roger?' I shrugged. 'He chickened out on me back at the studio.'

'No, he didn't,' she said firmly. 'I hit him on the head with a frying pan and put him in the trunk ... so he wouldn't get hurt.'

I nodded, impressed. 'Makes perfect sense.'

My opinion of Jessica was growing by the minute.

'We're obviously not going anywhere in my car,' she said, gazing at the wreck. 'Let's take yours.'

But Dolores's Ford had vanished. I turned and walked into the middle of the street.

Along the road was a zigzagging tire track and strewn around it were the twisted metal of Toon-cycles, broken lampposts, the spilled contents of Toon shopping baskets wandering around in a daze. It wasn't hard to guess who the culprit was.

'I got a feeling somebody already took it. Hmm?' I said.

She got my drift. 'From the looks of it, I'd say it was Roger. My honey bunny was never very good behind the wheel.'

'A better lover than a driver, huh?'

She stopped and fixed me with one of her looks. 'You'd better believe it, buster,' she said, poking me in the chest, then looked over my shoulder and pulled a face. I turned round, and saw the Toon Squad paddy wagon roaring over the crest of a hill in the distance.

'Uh-oh,' Jessica sighed, 'it's the weasels! This way! We'll take Gingerbread Lane.'

'No, wait!' I said, resisting her efforts to drag me by the arm. 'No, no! Gingerbread Lane's this way.'

So we stood there tugging at each other for another few minutes and I was just wondering whether we might try something a bit more intimate than tugging when who should turn up but Benny.

'So, Valiant, you call a cab or what?'

I sighed, and then climbed into the driver's seat while Benny leered at Jessica as she ran round to the passenger's seat, shining his headlights on the contours of her amazing body as she wiggled past his front end.

'Hubba, hubba, hubba!' he honked, opening the door for her to climb in. 'Allow me, mademoiselle.'

'Oh, come on Benny!' I scolded him. 'Let's move!'

So once again I found myself being chased by four rather

silly Toons and putting my faith in one very crazy Toon.

We sped back towards Toontown Tunnel and soon were plunged back into darkness. It was time to get a few answers out of Jessica.

'So how long have you known it was Doom?'

'Before poor Marvin was killed, he confided to me that Doom wanted to get his hands on Toontown, and he wouldn't stop at anything.'

It figured. 'So he gave you the will for safe keeping?' I asked.

'That's what he told me. Except when I opened the envelope, there was only a blank piece of paper inside.'

'A joker to the end,' I muttered.

'So – where to, already,' said Benny cheerfully. 'My meter's runnin'.'

'I have to find my darling husband,' Jessica said. 'I'm so worried about him.' I guess by now I could tell that she meant it. To tell you the truth, I was worried about the rabbit myself, though don't ask me why. That was another question that needed answering.

'Seriously,' I said, 'what do you see in that guy?'

'He makes me laugh,' she said simply.

'Hey!' I shouted as Jessica and I were jerked back. We were emerging out of the other end of the tunnel and Benny had decided it was time to put on some speed. We shot around a bend and there was Doom standing by the side of the road. Next to him was the barrel labelled 'POISON: TURPEN-TINE'. As Benny tore towards him, I saw Doom grin horribly and kick the barrel over. The Dip seeped into the middle of the road and a moment later Benny was skidding into it, spinning us around.

'I've been dipped!' hooted Benny and as we all screamed he skidded off the road and smashed into a lamppost.

'Oh, no!' Jessica squealed as she and I were thrown out of our seats onto the side of the road.

'Ooohh!' sighed Benny through his exhaust as he collapsed under the broken lamppost that leaned down over him.

'Tsk, tsk, tsk, tsk, tsk,' said Doom, standing over us. 'What an unfortunate accident.'

117

He glanced along the road just as the Toon Squad paddy wagon emerged from the tunnel.

'Nothing more treacherous than a slippery road,' he said smoothly, 'and especially when driven in a maniacal Toon vehicle.'

The paddy wagon screeched to a stop before reaching the river of Dip and the weasels jumped out.

'Good work, boss,' piped Smart Ass, while Psycho and Wheezy sniggered and wheezed.

'Don't just stand there,' Doom snarled at his henchmen, 'help them. Put them in the car.'

I saw Benny open his eyes for an instant and peek at the weasels, then he shut them again, making out like he was unconscious.

'I think they'll enjoy attending the ribbon-cutting at the Gag Factory,' Doom shouted.

The elements must have been in cahoots with him that night, because a moment after he spoke there was a heavy roll of thunder and a flash of lightning that illuminated his chalky white face. If I hadn't suspected it already, one thing was now as clear as daylight.

Judge Doom was completely mad.

17

I was back inside the Gag Factory. Only this time there were no cops around and Doom held all the cards.

While Stupid and Wheezy jackhammered a hole in the wall, I'd been frisked a few times by the rest of the weasels. To be precise, they had poked and dug and tickled me, and Psycho kept on pinching me for kicks, so I kicked him for kicks. He fell backwards on the floor but got up again and kept right on pinching. It was ticklish but I wasn't laughing. They were having another go at me when Doom came riding down the wall on a vertical conveyor belt.

'We searched Valiant, boss,' said Smart Ass. 'The will ain't on him.'

'Then frisk the woman,' Doom snapped.

'*I'll* handle this one,' simpered Greasy, rubbing his hands. He stepped over to Jessica and stuck his arm down her cleavage – or rather up to her cleavage and then down, seeing as how she was twice his height – and pulled out a bear trap, which clamped down hard on his hand. He yelped and muttered in pain while the other weasels fell about in hysterics.

'Nice booby trap,' I said.

Doom stepped up to Greasy and hit him with his cane, knocking him back into a pile of boxes. A bunch of fake eyeballs spilled out and rolled around on the floor, sending Smart Ass, Psycho, Stupid and Wheezy into new fits of giggles until Doom spun around to glare at them and the factory lights dimmed.

'Do they have the will or not?' he thundered.

'No, boss,' Smart Ass replied, 'just a stupid love letter.'

'No matter,' Doom barked. 'I doubt if that will is going to show up in the next fifteen minutes anyway.'

I snatched the rabbit's love letter back from Psycho and tucked it in my jacket pocket.

'What happens in the next fifteen minutes?' I said.

'Toontown'll be legally mine,' Doom replied, 'lock, stock and barrel.'

Benny opened his eyes. From deep inside Toontown Tunnel came the clattering, clanking sound of a car in the last stages of disintegration; there was a grinding of gears and a shower of sparks and then Dolores's car appeared, reversing out of the tunnel with Roger Rabbit at the wheel. The car spun around and crashed into the curb.

'Benny!' shouted Roger Rabbit, standing up in the car to get a better look. 'Is that you?'

The Toon cab slipped out from under the lamppost which leaned down even further over the road.

'No, it's Shirley Temple!' he groaned, then stood up on his melted rear tires and tiptired painfully towards the Ford. 'Ahh! Oh! Eee!' he moaned.

'Jumpin' jeepers!' Roger exclaimed, leaning his head out of the Ford. 'What happened?'

'Doom grabbed your wife and Valiant and took 'em to the Gag Factory!' Benny honked.

'The Gag Factory? I know where that is. Get in!' Roger opened the door and Benny climbed into the driver's seat.

'Move over, Rog,' he said. 'You've done enough drivin' for one night.'

He switched on his own headlights and began to drive

Dolores's Ford down the road towards the factory. When it came down to it, the story of who framed Roger Rabbit was one of wheels within wheels.

As they arrived at the factory Roger pulled out a pistol and leapt out of the car.

'Benny,' he whispered. 'You go for the cops. I'm gonna save my wife.'

Benny dipped his headlights and cringed as Roger waved the pistol around.

'Be careful with that gun!' he warned. 'This ain't no cartoon, ya know!'

As the truth of this dawned on him, Roger began quivering and whimpering with fear, and climbed back into the car to hide.

'This is no way to make a living,' muttered Benny, shoving the rabbit out of the car.

Roger crept over to a basement window and struggled, huffing and puffing, to raise it. He finally gave up and leaned against the glass.

'Wouldn't you know?' he sighed. 'Locked.'

As he spoke the window flipped open under his weight and he tumbled through it, falling head first into a toilet bowl. For a brief moment his head reappeared out of the toilet, which then flushed, sucking him back down.

18

'Uh, Toontown right on the other side of the wall, boss.'
Stupid called out as he and Wheezy finished jackhammering
and stood back to survey their handiwork: multi-colored
sunlight was streaming through the hole from Toontown on
the other side. I can't say the bluebirds over the rainbow filled
me with much joy but then I hadn't been in much of a mood to
follow the yellow brick road in the first place.

'You see, Mr Valiant?' said Doom smugly. 'The successful
conclusion of this case draws the curtains on my career as jurist
in Toontown.'

He was walking across the factory towards this large tent-
shaped tarpaulin.

'I'm retiring to take a new role in the private sector.'

'That wouldn't be Cloverleaf Industries by any chance,
huh?' I said.

'Eh, eh!' growled Smart Ass, pointing a gun at me and
pushing me back. Doom just smiled.

'You're looking at the sole stockholder.'

I should have guessed. Blame it on the whiskey.

He dropped a silver tray in front of the tarpaulin, then
pulled back a flap to reveal a funnel-shaped faucet.

'Can you guess what this is?'

More guessing games. This time I knew the answer but as I didn't think Doom would be handing out prizes I kept quiet. Jessica didn't, though.

'Oh, my God!' she screamed as he turned on the faucet and turpentine poured out into the silver tray. 'It's Dip!'

'That's right, my dear!' he grinned. 'Enough to dip Toontown off the face of the Earth!'

He pulled down the rest of the tarpaulin. I could now see what looked like a gigantic streetcleaning truck, only he'd rigged it up here and there with some fancy bits and pieces so it would function as a Dip sprayer.

'A vehicle of my own design. Five thousand gallons of heated Dip, pumped at enormous velocity through a pressurized water cannon.'

While Psycho climbed up a ramp to the water cannon perched at the top, Wheezy stood perched on the edge of the truck's enormous vat and poured in some 'MENTHYL-ATED SPIRITS' from a barrel; Stupid was pushing another barrel up a ladder, and Psycho was preparing the cannon. As for Smart Ass, he was holding Jessica and me at gunpoint, so you could say everyone had his hands tied except Doom – but he was doing the talking.

'Toontown will be erased in a matter of minutes,' he finished.

'I suppose you think no one's going to notice Toontown's disappeared?' Jessica said bravely.

He snorted. 'Who's got the time to wonder what happened to some ridiculous talking mice when you're driving by at *seventy miles an hour*!'

Jessica and I stared at each other.

'What are you talking about?' she said. 'There's no road past Toontown.'

'Not yet!' he said, rubbing his long bony hands. He walked away from the truck and nearly stumbled over the fake eyeballs. It was good while it lasted.

'Several months ago,' he went on, regaining his balance, 'I had the good providence to stumble upon a plan of the city council. A construction plan of epic proportions. They are calling it...' he paused and held his head aloft dramatically '...a freeway!'

'A freeway?' I repeated, foxed. 'What the hell's a freeway?'

Doom started to walk towards me. 'Eight lanes of shimmering cement running from here to Pasadena. Smooth, safe, fast. Traffic jams will be a thing of the past.'

So that's what Maroon had been trying to tell me: *Toontown's gonna be land for the free.* The poor bastard never got to say what kind of free.

'And that's why you killed Marvin and Maroon? For this freeway?' I said. 'I don't get it.'

Doom smiled. 'Of course not. You lack vision.' He walked away towards the far end of the factory, like he was Napoleon replanning Waterloo. 'But I see a place where people get on and off the freeway! On and off! Off and on! All day! All night.'

He stopped at the end of the factory and turned back to us. 'Soon,' he said, pointing his cane at the hole in the Toontown wall, 'where Toontown once stood there will be...'

He paused and we waited to hear what wonders he was conjuring up.

'... a string of gas stations, inexpensive motels, restaurants that serve rapidly prepared food, tire stores, automobile dealerships and... wonderful, wonderful billboards –' He stopped and raised his arms heavenwards.

'– reaching as far as the eye can see! My God! It'll be beautiful.'

'Come on,' I said. 'Nobody's gonna drive this lousy freeway when they can take the Red Car for a nickel.'

'They'll drive,' he cried in a thundering voice. 'They'll have to. You see... I bought the Red Car so I could dismantle it.'

He stopped abruptly. From below us the floor had begun to rumble like the beginnings of an earthquake.

'What the –' Smart Ass began.

Suddenly a geyser of water burst through the drainage gate under which Greasy had been standing, sending him shooting up into the air.

124

I couldn't believe what I was seeing. It was just like another of those crazy Maroon cartoons.

Dancing around in the jet of water on which Greasy was suspended... was the rabbit.

While Roger screamed and flailed his arms around, kind of cycling inside the geyser, the water was showering in all directions – on the weasels, Jessica and me and Doom himself.

Doom stepped back from the shower just as the geyser began to lose its power. As it receded, Greasy started to fall, but just in time he grabbed hold of a net full of bricks which was hanging from the ceiling with the sign 'BRICKS: ONE TON' attached to it.

'Caramba!' the weasel shrieked.

Roger Rabbit just fell straight down, his mouth wide open in a piercing scream as he plummeted from the ceiling to the floor of the factory.

This was the rabbit's finest hour and he wasn't wasting it. He landed, incredibly, feet first on the floor and instantly pointed a pistol at the Judge.

'OK, nobody move!' he cried as Smart Ass and Psycho started to move in on him with their guns. 'All right, weasels, grab some sky or I let the Judge have it.' He turned and pointed his gun at the weasels. 'You heard me, I said drop it!'

Smart Ass dropped his gun.

'Roger, darling!' Jessica gasped, beside herself with joy.

He leaped to her side like one of the Three Musketeers.

'Yes, it's me, my dearest,' he cried. 'I'd love to embrace you, but *first*...' he turned and re-aimed his gun at Psycho and Smart Ass '... I have to satisfy my sense of moral outrage!'

'Put that gun down, you buck-toothed fool!' stormed the Judge, taking a step towards him.

'That's it, Doom,' Roger shouted, waving the gun around, and forcing Doom to step back again. 'Give me another excuse to pump you full of lead!'

Greasy snapped open a switchblade knife as he dangled from the net of bricks.

'You thought you could get away with it, didn't you?' Roger shrieked. 'Ha! We Toons may act idiotic, but we're not stupid.

We demand justice.'

The rabbit had forced Doom back past the drainage gate while he himself had stopped on top of it.

'Why, the real meaning of the word probably hits you like a ton of bricks!' he added.

As he spoke, the ton of bricks, released from the net by Greasy's switchblade, fell on top of him.

Greasy, hung from his rope shrieking with laughter, and the other weasels joined in.

'Roger!' Jessica screamed, running over to kneel down beside the pile of bricks.

The rabbit poked his head up out of the bricks and lolled about looking dopey as stars encircled his head.

At least they weren't birds or fish.

'Roger, say something,' Jessica cried anxiously.

He came out of his stupor and gazed around him, then pointed upwards. 'Look, stars!' he giggled happily. 'Ready when you are, Raoul.'

'Tie the lovebirds together,' Doom commanded.

He walked over to the wall and picked up a control box, pressing the 'Down' button, while the weasels bumped into each other and squabbled over who should tie what end of which length of rope to which one of the Toons. Finally Doom settled the matter.

'Put them on that hook!' he snapped.

Smart Ass was still holding me at gunpoint as the other weasels herded Jessica and Roger over to a large hook which was descending from the ceiling. Stupid, Wheezy and Greasy tied them to the hook.

'Use that escape-proof Toon rope,' ordered the Judge.

The weasels pulled out a length of rope from a crate and there was something about that rope that sent a chill through my body.

Psycho climbed up a ladder to the water cannon above the truck. 'Time to kill the rabbit,' he shrieked.

Roger and Jessica Rabbit were now strung up on the hook like chickens. Doom pressed the 'Up' button on his control box and the hook started to rise, dragging the Rabbits up towards the ceiling.

'Oh, Roger,' Jessica sighed, 'you were magnificent.'

The rabbit looked abashed. 'Was I really?'

Jessica fluttered her lashes. 'Better than Goofy.'

Greasy turned the key of the ignition and pressed his foot down on the accelerator.

Steam began to pour out of the engine of the Dip truck and Wheezy climbed up the ladder towards the cannon. The mixer began to turn in the Dip vat.

'Roger, darling,' Jessica said, looking into his dopey eyes. 'I want you to know I love you. I've loved you more than any woman's ever loved a rabbit.'

19

'It's over, Mr Valiant,' said the Judge, walking towards me with a smug grin on his chalky face – and tripped once again on the eyeballs.

This time they sent him reeling all over the floor.

The weasels broke into paroxysms of giggles while Doom made continuous efforts to stand up. But each time the eyeballs got the better of him and he slid back down again.

It was just what I needed. I warily took a step forward as Smart Ass held his sides and roared with laughter. Doom, lying on his stomach, saw what I was up to and holding a hand over one eye, he stretched out his other hand to point up at me.

'Look out!' he shouted at Smart Ass, but at the same moment I reached out to grab the weasel.

'You fools!' Doom groaned.

Abruptly Smart Ass stopped laughing and pointed his gun at my nose. 'Not so fast,' he hissed.

Reluctantly I held my hands up.

'One of these days,' the Judge snarled, as he got back to his feet, 'you idiots are gonna laugh yourselves to death!'

'Shall I repose of him right now, boss?' said Smart Ass.

Doom stood up, with one hand still over his eye.

'Let him watch his Toon friends get dipped,' he snapped, covering up his eye with both hands, 'then shoot him.'

'With pleasure,' the weasel replied.

For no reason that I could see, this sent the other weasels off into a further round of hysterics and Greasy, up in the truck cab, leaned back as he laughed and accidentally pushed down the emergency brake and then trod on the clutch.

'Everything's funny to you, ain't it, needle nose,' I growled at Smart Ass.

The weasel definitely didn't like this. 'You got a problem with that, Valiant?' he snarled, pushing me backwards with the barrel of his gun against the calliope.

A laugh can be a very powerful thing. Why, sometimes in life, it's the only weapon we have.

I didn't have a problem with the weasels' laughing. In fact, it might just be doing me and the Toons a big, big favor. That and the calliope. It had been a long time – nearly forty years – since me and Teddy and Dad had toured with Barnum and Bailey, but it's a bit like learning how to ride a bike. Once you're a clown you never forget how to do it.

I reached backwards for a lever on the calliope.

'No,' I chuckled. 'I just, uh . . . want you to know something about the guy you're gonna dip.'

I found the calliope lever and pushed it upwards. There was a panel on the front which read:

SELECT-A-TUNE
JOLSON MEDLEY
MERRY-GO-ROUND BROKE DOWN
BROADWAY SELECTION
MICKEY'S MELODY
STARS AND STRIPS FOREVER

I pressed the button next to 'Merry-Go-Round Broke Down'. Instantly it lit up and started to play. The weasel was thrown into confusion.

'Eh . . . eh, eh . . . eh, eh . . . ehh!' he gasped, backing away from the calliope.

Up on the Dip truck the other weasels stared down, completely distracted – which, of course, was the whole idea.

So then I started to sing and dance along with the calliope:

> *'Now Roger is his name,*
> *Laughter is his game.*
> *Come on, you dope,*
> *Untie his rope*
> *And watch him go in –'*

As I sang the last word I reached the other side of the calliope and jumped on a broom. It sprang back, hitting me on the head.

> *'– sane!'*

The weasels were in total confusion. Stupid even climbed up a ladder on the side of the truck to get a better view.

I turned around and leaped into the air, wiggling my feet in mid-air and landing on the base of the broom, so that the handle hit me in the back and knocked me to the floor; then I somersaulted back in front of the calliope, landing on my rear and skidding to a stop in front of Smart Ass.

The weasel couldn't help himself. He started to laugh, which set off the other weasels, who began writhing around in hysterics. Meanwhile I was trying out a few reverse handsprings. That's something I hadn't done since the LAPD Police Academy days, but I found I could do them perfectly. And I've got to tell you this: Dad would have been proud of me – and so would Teddy.

'He's lost his mind,' said Jessica.

'I don't think so,' replied the rabbit with a wink.

I took three gag bombs out of a crate and carried them across the floor; then I danced in place – kicking my legs on the spot and stepping back each time.

> *'This singin' ain't my line.*

If I get stuck I'm . . .
I'm out of luck and
Um . . . uh . . . uh . . .'

I'd forgotten the words, but Jessica came to my rescue:
'I'm running out of time!' she sang out to me.

'Thanks!' I shouted, throwing the bombs up in the air.

One by one they landed on my head and I followed this up
by slipping on a banana skin.

'Whoa!' I wailed, and fell against some boxes, disappearing
from view.

'Aagh!'

By this time the weasels were doubled up with laughter.

I leaped out from the pile of boxes on a pogo stick and
bounced across the floor, each time flying higher until finally I
crashed into a ceiling lamp and hung from it, dropping the
pogo stick to the floor. Then I screamed as the lamp gave me
an electric shock, and sparks flew in all directions.

This was too much for Stupid to take. He fell back off the
ladder and collapsed in hysterics on the floor.

The lamp stopped sparking and I let go, falling to the floor –
which was enough to finish Stupid off. Lying on the floor he
expired, his body stiffening. A Toon lily appeared in his hands
and then his Toon ghost rose into the air, while the calliope
began playing funeral organ music.

My next victim was Wheezy, who fell back laughing on the
ladder. To his astonishment his ghost started rising up out of
him before he'd even copped it. Still laughing uncontrollably,
he tried to pull the ghost back, until the ladder backed away
from the wall, so that it was precariously upright.

'Hey, Eddie, keep it up!' the rabbit shouted across to me.
'You're killin' em! You're slayin' em! You're knockin' 'em
dead.'

Wheezy's ghost had broken free of his body's grasp and flew
upwards towards the ceiling. Wheezy himself was still
laughing and then the end of his ladder fell back against a rope,
loosening it from the wall cleat. The rope released a fifty ton
weight, which fell onto a seesaw, and a box of iron balls

catapulted off the other end of the seesaw. The balls fell against a conveyor belt control lever, activating the belt, which then carried a vase forward.

Meanwhile, as the funeral musical changed back to calliope music, I launched into another verse:

> *'I'm through with takin' falls*
> *And bouncin' off the walls.*
> *Without that gun*
> *I'd have some fun.*
> *I'd kick you in the –'*

I was about to finish the song by kicking Wise Ass where it rhymed, when the vase rose to the top of the conveyor belt, tumbled over and smashed on my head, knocking me over.

'– Nose!' the rabbit completed for me obligingly.

'"Nose"?' Smart Ass shouted up at him. 'That don't rhyme with "walls".'

'No,' I said, getting back on my feet, 'but this does.'

And then I kicked him in the nuts.

'He-e-e-lp!' he squealed, and went flying up into the air . . . and landed in the vat of Dip.

Psycho and Greasy screeched with laughter. Greasy laughed so much he choked to death and fell out of the door of the truck cab. His foot, slipping off the clutch, released it and the truck shifted into gear and began to move as Greasy's ghost rose up from the cab.

While Psycho was still laughing hysterically, his hand accidentally flipped up the cannon lever to maximum power and Dip started to shoot out of the cannon nozzle, narrowly missing the Rabbits and hitting the wall behind them.

'Yikes!' they screamed and tried to swing out of the way of the spray.

'Oh, my goodness!' Roger yelped.

'Oh, Roger!' Jessica screeched.

Psycho meanwhile had fallen off the water cannon platform and, grabbing the steering lever, he pulled it down with him.

'Jeepers . . .' the rabbit squealed as the cannon nozzle began to swivel and the spray moved away from them, '... that was close!'

Psycho laughed so hard he let go of the cannon lever and fell screaming into one of the truck's roller brushes. His ghost rose up from the roller brush and flew up the cannon.

'Bye, bye!' it screamed with maniacal laughter. It hovered next to the cannon and then pushed the steering lever in the opposite direction. The cannon swivelled back to its former position so that Roger and Jessica were once more about to fall directly in the path of the spray.

'Eddie!' the rabbit shrieked. 'Hurry! It's coming back!'

I ran around one of the brushes and started to climb up the cannon ladder as the spray of Dip remorselessly moved towards Roger and Jessica Rabbit.

20

I reached the top of the ladder and crawled along the cannon platform. I could see Doom opposite me riding up the vertical conveyor belt. Roger and Jessica were screaming and squirming, as they tried to wriggle away from the Dip spray as it closed on them.

'This is it!' Roger sobbed.

I reached the cannon leaver and pushed it. The spray moved away again.

'This *isn't* it,' the rabbit sighed.

I looked up and saw Doom using his cane to slide down a wire towards me. He reached the platform and lunged at me, kicking me in the chest and knocking me off the platform. I tumbled through the air and fell behind some boxes. Doom too fell off the platform, landing on his feet. I put up my fists, prepared to fight it out in the old-fashioned way, when to my alarm he pulled out a sword from his cane sheath and aimed it at me. He moved towards me and I was forced backwards. Then I noticed a box with the label: 'SINGING SWORDS'.

I darted down and opened the box, removing a Toon sword which bent and wriggled until, to my astonishment, it turned into a silver Frank Sinatra face. I stepped forward to parry with the sword and, incredibly, it began to sing like Sinatra, wriggling Frankie's adam's apple and lips:

> 'Wicked witchcraft,
> And although I know
> It's slightly taboo...'

For a moment Doom lowered his guard, instinctively disarmed by Young Blue Eyes' voice, then he smiled, stepped forward and raised his sword again. When I realised that Frank wasn't going to help me now, I threw him away, and instead pulled from another crate a giant cartoon magnet. I aimed it at Doom and magnetic rays shot out and grabbed his sword. He tried to resist but the magnet was sucking not just the sword but Doom himself towards me. Too close, in fact, for comfort. I pointed the magnet down and the magnetism kind of switched off.

Without thinking I held the magnet around my waist and it began to pull me down on to the floor. Then to my alarm a metal barrel slammed into my back, trapping the magnet around my chest.

'Don't move,' Doom snapped, re-sheathing his sword.

It didn't seem like I had much choice.

While all this was going on, the wheels of the truck were slowly rolling on to a pile of bricks. The rabbit and Jessica were screaming as the truck moved towards them and I was trying to break free of that magnet. I looked over to my right and saw a steamroller driving towards me, with Doom sitting at the wheel.

My efforts to get out of the magnet grew frantic.

'No!' I screamed. 'No! No! No!'

As the steamroller moved towards me Doom was leaning over the side to get a better view.

It was now just a few feet away from me. I looked round desperately for a way to escape. Then I saw it. There was a pile of boxes just out of reach. All I needed to do was to get hold of one of them. I stretched out my foot and kicked.

The boxes scattered.

I groaned and muttered a curse, kicking and groping as the steamroller closed in on me. At the last moment I whisked one out with my shoe and it rolled near enough for me to grab it. I placed the black circle on the front of the magnet and scrambled out through the hole.

Doom, was still leaning over the side, grinning in anticipation of imminent gore. Then I saw a puzzled, cheated look come over his face when he realised I was no longer there. It cheered me up no end.

I climbed on to the steamroller. Doom was now peering around the factory, baffled at my disappearing act. I crept up behind him, waited for him to turn around and then lifted my leg back and kicked Doom hard in the face. He grunted, fell back out of his seat, and tumbled out onto the floor, landing on his back. I leaped off the steamroller and got ready for another fight as Doom climbed to his feet.

I aimed a right hook – and missed. Doom retaliated with a left – and landed it, sending me hurtling across the floor. I saw him smiling with triumph as the steamroller, still in gear, moved towards me once more, knocking over a desk in its path.

I grabbed the nearest thing I could see, which happened to be a can of glue, raised it over my head and tried to hit him with it, but Doom put his hands out and gripped the other side of it. For a minute we did a kind of dance round the glue can, spinning and twirling. It was almost cosy.

Then Doom spoiled the fun by letting go and punching me on the nose instead.

I grunted in pain and, still holding the glue can, staggered back against the steamroller. Then he came at me, punching me in the face and chest. I tried to block the punches with the can of glue and his fist smashed into it.

Disgusted and horrified, he pulled back his hand: the glue can was stuck fast to his fist. He shook his fist and the can slid off, trailing a long string of glue. It rolled on the floor spilling glue next to his legs. I watched him draw his arm back, preparing to hit me with his glue-covered fist.

I ducked at the crucial moment and his fist smashed into the steamroller. He howled and tried to pull it away but the glue had stuck fast. He stepped back and his foot landed in a puddle of glue.

Up on the hook the Rabbits were squealing as the Dip spray moved back towards them and Doom was grunting and groaning as he tried to free his hand. He managed to lift his foot out of the puddle of glue and rammed it against the steamroller to get better leverage. At last he freed his hand from the roller, but then he got his foot stuck.

I turned and ran towards the Dip truck.

'Come on, Eddie!' the rabbit shouted. 'Quit playing around!'

I grabbed the truck door handle and climbed inside as the spray slowly angled itself towards the Rabbits who were shrieking and wailing.

'P-p-p-please!' the rabbit screamed.

'He-e-e-lp!' Jessica squealed.

I reached inside the truck and turned off the cannon. In seconds the Dip spray subsided.

The rabbit instantly started giggling. 'I wasn't worried,' he said to Jessica. 'Were you?'

I climbed out of the truck and staggered towards Doom.

His foot, which had been stuck to the roller, was now *caught under* it.

'Whoooooooooooooooooo! Whooooooooooooooo!' he howled as the roller pushed him back.

'Whooooooooooooooooooooooooooooooo!'

The roller moved over his legs and crushed them beneath it.

'Whoooooooooooooooooo!'

I stared with disbelief as his torso disappeared underneath the roller, then his chest, then . . .

I turned away in horror.

'Yecch!' as the rabbit put it so aptly.

I heard a crunching noise as the head and neck of the late Judge Doom were flattened by the steamroller.

I was feeling rather queasy, but at least it was all over.

'Hey, look!' Roger shouted.

I ventured a glance at the roller and then stared in equal helpings of horror and fascination.

The roller had left behind a kind of black, flattened, two-dimensional version of Doom, like a paper cutout. But that wasn't all. *The cutout Doom began to raise its arms and started to get up.*

21

It sprang to its feet and staggered back and forth.

'Holy smoke!' I gasped. 'He's a Toon!'

'Surprised?' said Doom, turning to me.

'Not really,' I said. 'That lame-brained freeway idea could only be cooked up by a Toon.'

'Not just any Toon!' he said, and staggered over to an air tank.

His flat hand turned on the pump and his other hand began to inflate; then his feet inflated and righted themselves. He pumped air into his mouth: his hat and chest expanded until his hat flew off his head. His glass eyes fell on to the floor by his feet.

Finally he turned round and looked at me.

I gasped.

His eyes were the bulging, red cartoon eyes of a demented lunatic.

'Remember me, Eddie?'

He began walking towards me.

'When I killed your brother, I talked...'

His voice rose to a piercing, high-pitched screech.

'... just ... like ... thi-i-i-i-i-i-i-s!'

His eyes suddenly turned into daggers. I was shocked – and terrified. I backed away slowly, then turned and ran. I looked around and saw cartoon springs suddenly appear on Doom's feet. He leaped into the air and flew at me, grabbing me from behind, spinning me around.

'Jumpin' jeepers!' I heard the rabbit gasp, then Doom smashed an iron fist into me and I fell on my back.

He opened the door of the truck, reached inside and turned on the cannon nozzle.

The Dip spray began to shoot out of the cannon again.

'Oh, my goodness!' Jessica screamed.

'Yikes!' shrieked the rabbit.

I got back to my feet and was about to brave another assault on Doom when he spun round and pulled off his glove to reveal a cartoon anvil where there should have been a hand. He lashed at me, sending me hurtling to the floor again. I landed beside the ton of bricks and slid ten feet across the floor.

He turned away from me for a second and then turned back. The anvil had turned into a huge, cartoon buzzsaw. He pointed it at me and began walking towards me. With every step the buzzsaw arm grew in size until it filled my vision.

I lay on my back, petrified as Doom held his buzzsaw arm over his head. To give me a taste of its lethal power he pointed it at a large, vicious-looking chain hanging from the ceiling. Sparks flew from the chain and in seconds he cut through it like scissors through paper and it fell clanging to the floor.

Then he pointed his buzzsaw arm back at me, advancing on me and lashing and flailing the buzzsaw like a whip and grinning hideously. Suddenly his eyes changed again, this time into spirals. He lowered the buzzsaw towards my stomach and lunged for me, but I twisted out of the way and the buzzsaw cut into the floor, sending sparks flying.

I rolled out of the way and grabbed the Toon mallet which had fallen out of the broken desk. As he thrust the buzzsaw at me again I pointed the mallet at him, but ducked out of the way so that the buzzsaw ripped through the desk.

Doom pulled back the buzzsaw and this time before he could lunge I pressed the button on the mallet. The boxing glove sprang out and shot past him; instead, it hit the release lever on the Dip truck, then it retracted, whizzing past him and returning to the mallet.

'Huh?' Doom stared at the retreating glove, and then screamed in horror as the spray of Dip shot out of the truck and landed on him.

Knocked back by the force of the spray, he collapsed on the floor. The Dip spray kept on rising up towards Roger and Jessica and they too began to scream again.

'Goodbye, my darling,' Jessica sighed. 'Goodbye!'

The spray which had been gushing out at maximum velocity suddenly subsided until it was just a trickle.

'I think I'm gonna faint,' Jessica gasped.

I stood up, tossing the mallet aside. I could see Doom standing in a flood of Dip as the last of it shot out of the vat in the truck. He was screeching and yelling as it washed over his feet, yellow smoke rising from the Dip as he began to melt.

'I'm me-l-l-l-l-l-ting!' he screamed. 'Whooooooooo!'

He started to sink into the Dip as smoke engulfed him.

'Whoo-whoooooooooooooo! Melting!'

In no time at all he had disappeared for ever, melting completely back into the foul miasma that had been created by the warped hand and brain of a Toon gone wrong.

22

Then I remembered the Rabbits.

Dip was still coming out of the cannon. It may have just been a trickle but it was enough to put an end for ever to the careers of Maroon Cartoons' leading star and the toast of the Ink and Paint Club, because the Dip truck itself was slowly rolling towards them.

'Eddie!' Roger was screaming.

'Help!' shrieked Jessica.

'Hurry up! Do something!'

I ran across the Dip-covered floor to the power winch control box and grabbed the controls as the Rabbits tried desperately to swing away from the truck. It was mere inches away from them as I pressed the button.

The power winch hoisted them clear of the oncoming truck, which, seconds later, crashed into the wall and broke through into Toontown on the other side.

All at once the air was filled with chirping and whistling and the sound of music. As the truck moved onto the Toontown countryside it collided with a cartoon express train. Then a Toon push cart passed by with a pig and buzzard inside.

Roger Rabbit, still hanging with Jessica from the hook

stared at the hole in the wall next to them.

'Eddie, there's Dip everywhere!' the rabbit reminded me – as if I needed reminding – 'How are we gonna get down?'

I glanced around the factory and spotted a fire hydrant main valve sign. I walked over to it and turned on the valve. Water gushed out of a hydrant, drenching me. Then, all over the factory, water gushed out from the hydrants, flooding the Dip and washing it down into the drains.

Once the Dip had been washed away, I pressed the winch control again, lowering Roger and Jessica slowly to the ground. I ran across the factory and untied them.

'Jeepers, Eddie!' sighed the rabbit. 'That was a close shave! I thought for sure our goose was cooked.'

'Oh!' Jessica gasped as I helped her down from the winch, 'My hero.'

I smiled modestly and chuckled. It was nice to be appreciated.

So I guess I was a little disgruntled when she walked past me and gave the rabbit a huge hug.

'Honey bunny,' she sighed.

'Oh, love cups,' he giggled.

Then she picked him up and planted a dozen kisses on his rabbity cheeks.

'Oh, Roger! You were a pillar of strength.'

I turned away in disgust.

From outside the factory came the sound of a police siren and then Santino's car, Benny the Toon cab and a police car roared into the factory. They came to a halt by the gory black remains of Judge Doom.

'Sister Mary Francis!' hooted Benny, shining his headlights on Doom's remains. 'What the hell happened in here? I've been a cab for thirty-seven years, and I've never seen a mess like this!'

Through the hole into Toontown came a general buzz of chattering, chirping, giggles and whistles as the entire cartoon population appeared to have gathered to peek through into the factory.

I went over to Dolores who had arrived with Santino. We

kissed and she clucked over my various bumps and bruises. I didn't mind. To tell the truth, I thought I deserved a little love and affection at that moment.

'What was that?' she asked, grimacing at the muck that had been the maniac Toon. 'A rubber mask?'

'Yeah.'

I turned to Santino and picked up the rope that Doom and the weasels had used to tie up the Rabbits. 'And this is the rope from the safe that was dropped on Marvin. Same rope Doom used when he dropped the piano on my brother.' I tossed the rope to Santino, then I rejoined Dolores and held her hand.

'I think your lab boys will find that paint's a perfect match.'

Santino looked down distastefully at Doom's remains. 'Judge Doom killed Marvin?'

'And R.K. Maroon. And my brother.'

'That's what I call one seriously disturbed Toon,' he muttered.

Dolores nudged me and pointed at the hole in the wall. Toontown's residents were paying us a social visit – or rather, they'd come for the post-mortem. I'd never seen so many familiar Toons in one place before: the Road Runner, Bambi, Betty Boop, Mickey Mouse and Bugs Bunny (with whom I still had a few scores to settle), Minnie Mouse, Daffy Duck, Pinocchio, Baby Herman, Donald Duck and Goofy. I almost wished I'd brought my autograph book.

They gathered round the death mask. 'I wonder who he really was,' said Mickey Mouse.

'I'll tell you one thing, Doc,' said Bugs Bunny. 'He weren't no rabbit.'

'Or a duck!' said Daffy.

And then all the other Toons chimed in. And all the time more Toons were joining the party. I saw the Big Bad Wolf wearing a sheep's costume, until he pulled off the sheep's head to reveal himself. And then there was Woody Woodpecker and Sylvester the Cat. Luckily Tweety Bird and her little piggies had stayed at home.

And, like I said, Dolores kept clucking over me like a mother hen, telling me I needed a bath and a shave and a haircut. And then she pointed to my shirt.

'What's that? What is that?'

'It's ink,' I said. 'That goof Marvin squirted me with some the other night. Why it's comin' out now, I don't know.'

'Here's your answer, Eddie,' said the rabbit. He'd taken a bottle out of one of the 'TRICK INK' boxes. The label read:

DISAPPEARING
&
RE-APPEARING
INK

'Boy,' he sighed, 'that Marvin, what a genius!'

'Applesauce!' came a scornful growl from somewhere around my feet.

I looked down and there was a big cigar with Baby Herman at the end of it.

'If he was such a genius,' he elaborated, 'why didn't he leave his will where we could find it? Without it, we're just waitin' for another developer's wrecking ball.'

I'd just had a ridiculous idea. I fiddled around in my pockets and pulled out Roger's love letter that the weasels had frisked out of me – before I'd frisked it back again.

'Roger,' I said.

'Yeah?' said the rabbit.

'That love letter you wrote to your wife in the Ink and Paint Club . . . why don't you read it to her now?'

I handed him the letter.

He looked delighted. 'Sure, Eddie.'

He unfolded the letter, preparing for his Big Performance. Romeo Rabbit.

'"Dear Jessica",' he read. '"How do I love thee? Let me count the ways. I, Marvin the Gag King, being of sound mind and body –" It's the will!' he shrieked.

And all around us the Toons broke into excited chattering, gasps and exclamations.

'Keep reading,' I ordered.

'"... do hereby bequeath, in perpetuity, the property

145

known as Toontown to those lovable characters, the Toons"!'

A loud cheer went up. Toons hugged each other, Dolores hugged me. Jessica hugged Roger. Santino hugged Benny. And Baby Herman hugged his cigar.

Dolores was just about to kiss me when the rabbit broke in, pulling me to one side.

'Hey, Eddie! That was a pretty, funny dance you did for the weasels. Do you think your days of bein' a sourpuss are over?'

'Only time will tell,' I grinned.

'Yeah, well, put it there, pal!'

'Yeah.'

I shook his hand.

Bzzzzzzzzzzzzzzzzzzzzzzzzzzzzz!

It was that goddamn handbuzzer again.

The Toons broke into fits of giggles. Roger sneaked a look at me.

I wasn't smiling. In fact, I glared at him.

He swallowed hard. 'Don't tell me you lost your sense of humor already?'

I took a deep breath, grimacing, and reached for the rabbit, grabbing him by the neck. He began to choke.

'Does this answer your question?' I said and then I grinned and gave him a big wet kiss on the lips.

'Oh, please!' he spluttered in a muffled voice, trying to pull away. Then, 'Blecch!' he spat, as he managed to release himself.

The Toons all cheered, jumping up and down with joy.

Jessica was looking broody. She picked up the rabbit and said huskily, 'Come on, Roger, let's go home.' Then she gave him a sultry look with half-closed eyes. 'I'll bake you a carrot cake.'

Roger Rabbit went all pink and chuckled as Jessica put him back down on the floor. Then, singing 'Smile Darn Ya Smile' along with all the other Toons, they took the hole-in-the-wall-route back to Toontown.

As for Dolores and me, well, I didn't figure we'd get far in the Ford, so when Benny flashed his headlights and said, 'So, Valiant, you call a cab or what?' I considered the proposal and looked at Dolores.

'Thanks, Benny,' she said, 'but we'll take a raincheck. Eddie and I need a walk.'

The Toon cab grinned and winked his headlight.

'No sweat.'

STAR BOOKS BESTSELLERS

	DAVID DEUTSCH	
0352319488	**The Equalizer**	£1.95*
0352319496	**The Equalizer 2**	£1.95*
035232189X	**The Equálizer 3**	£1.99*
	IAN DON	
0352320354	**Tough Guys**	£1.95*
	STEPHEN GRAVE	
0352316985	**Miami Vice 2: The Vengeance Game**	£1.95*
0352317590	**Miami Vice 3: The Razor's Edge**	£1.95*
0352317671	**Miami Vice 4: China White**	£1.95*
0352320222	**Miami Vice 5: Probing by Fire**	£1.95*
0352320451	**Miami Vice 6: Helhole**	£1.95*

STAR BOOKS BESTSELLERS

		SHAUN HUTSON	
△	0352316454	**Terminator**	£2.50
		GRAHAM MASTERTON	
△	0352396164	**The Manitou**	£1.50*
		PAUL MONETTE	
△	0352321466	**Predator**	£2.25
		MARTIN NOBLE	
△	0352320265	**Ruthless People**	£1.95
△	0352320818	**Tin Men**	£1.95
		ELAINE ROCHE	
△	0352320109	**Chateauvallon 1: The Berg Family Fortune**	£2.50

STAR Books are obtainable from many booksellers and newsagents. If you have any difficulty tick the titles you want and fill in the form below.

Name _____

Address _____

_____

Send to: Star Books Cash Sales, P.O. Box 11, Falmouth, Cornwall, TR10 9EN.

Please send a cheque or postal order to the value of the cover price plus: UK: 55p for the first book, 22p for the second book and 14p for each additional book ordered to the maximum charge of £1.75.

BFPO and EIRE: 55p for the first book, 22p for the second book, 14p per copy for the next 7 books, thereafter 8p per book.

OVERSEAS: £1.00 for the first book and 25p per copy for each additional book.

While every effort is made to keep prices low, it is sometimes necessary to increase prices at short notice. Star Books reserve the right to show new retail prices on covers which may differ from those advertised in the text or elsewhere.

*NOT FOR SALE IN CANADA

STAR BOOKS BESTSELLERS

		CARL RUHEN	
△	0352317396	**Sons and Daughters 1**	£2.25
△	035231740X	**Sons and Daughters 2**	£1.95
△	0352319739	**Sons and Daughters 3**	£2.25
△	0352319879	**Sons and Daughters 4**	£2.25
△	0352320656	**Sons and Daughters 5**	£2.25
	0352321512	**Sons and Daughters 6**	£2.50
△	0352321083	**Neighbours**	£2.25*
△	0352321490	**Neighbours 2**	£2.25
△	0352322012	**Neighbours 3**	£2.50*
		CARL RUHEN	
△	0352321717	**Young Doctors**	£2.50
△	0352322020	**Young Doctors 2**	£2.50*

STAR Books are obtainable from many booksellers and newsagents. If you have any difficulty tick the titles you want and fill in the form below.

Name _____

Address _____

_____

Send to: Star Books Cash Sales, P.O. Box 11, Falmouth, Cornwall, TR10 9EN.

Please send a cheque or postal order to the value of the cover price plus:
UK: 55p for the first book, 22p for the second book and 14p for each additional book ordered to the maximum charge of £1.75.

BFPO and EIRE: 55p for the first book, 22p for the second book, 14p per copy for the next 7 books, thereafter 8p per book.

OVERSEAS: £1.00 for the first book and 25p per copy for each additional book.

While every effort is made to keep prices low, it is sometimes necessary to increase prices at short notice. Star Books reserve the right to show new retail prices on covers which may differ from those advertised in the text or elsewhere.

*NOT FOR SALE IN CANADA